THE GREEK'S CONVENIENT MISTRESS

BY
ANNIE WEST

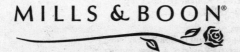
MILLS & BOON®

First published in Great Britain 2006
Paperback Edition 2007
Harlequin Mills & Boon Limited,
Eton House, 18-24 Paradise Road, Richmond, Surrey TW9 1SR

© Annie West 2006

ISBN-13: 978 0 263 85289 9
ISBN-10:   0 263 85289 X

Set in Times Roman 10 on 11¼ pt
01-0107-55988

Printed and bound in Spain
by Litografia Rosés, S.A., Barcelona

She took a single step, closing the gap so that the heat of his body encompassed hers.

She shivered, feeling as if she'd stepped into danger. The warm scent of his skin sent a jolt of desire right through her. She tilted her head up towards his. Her heartbeat raced as she saw his mouth, just a whisper of breath away from hers.

His lips had parted slightly, as if ready for the taste of her. Excitement twisted ever tighter in her belly, urging her on. She could kiss him if she just reached up and pressed her mouth against his.

He expected it too: the gleam in his eyes told her that.

Why? Why wait for her to make the first move? He must read the invitation in her eyes.

And then the answer came to her, like a bolt out of the clear sky, stabbing straight to her heart.

A shadow stood between them, a shade of the past. Costas looked at her, but, she realised, he didn't see her, not really. He was attracted to her because she reminded him of the woman he'd loved and lost just ten months ago. Her cousin, Fotini.

Annie West spent her childhood with her nose between the covers of a book—a habit she retains. After years preparing government reports and official correspondence, she decided to write something she *really* enjoys. And there's nothing she loves more than a great romance. Despite her office-bound past, she has managed a few interesting moments—including a marriage offer with the promise of a herd of camels to sweeten the contract. She is happily married to her ever-patient husband (who has never owned a dromedary). They live with their two children amongst the tall eucalypts at beautiful Lake Macquarie, on Australia's east coast. You can email Annie at www.annie-west.com

Recent titles by the same author:

A MISTRESS FOR THE TAKING

THE GREEK'S
CONVENIENT
MISTRESS

To Maureen,
for your wonderful generosity
in sharing so much.

To Karen,
for the tireless encouragement and hard work.

To Judy,
for advice on matters medical.

And to Dimitria,
whose Greek is so much better than mine.

Thank you all.

CHAPTER ONE

COSTAS SWITCHED OFF the ignition and studied the house he'd crossed the world to find. A red-brick bungalow in suburban Sydney. It was plain and solid, but with an air of recent neglect. Junk mail spilled from the letter box and the lawn was overgrown.

He frowned as he opened the car door and got out, stretching some of the stiffness from his tall frame.

Despite the uncollected mail he knew she was home. Or she had been thirty hours ago, before he'd left Athens. He refused to consider the possibility that she wasn't here. There was too much at stake to countenance failure.

Unclenching fingers that had curled into fists, he shrugged, trying to relieve the rigid set of his shoulders. He'd flown in first-class luxury as usual, but he'd been unable to sleep. The tension that had gripped him for so long now had reached crisis point. He hadn't slept for three days, had barely eaten.

He wouldn't rest till he got what he needed from this woman.

It took twenty seconds precisely to stride across the quiet street, through the low gateway and up the cement path to the front door.

He jabbed the doorbell and cast an assessing gaze across the tiny, unswept patio to the lacy cobwebs blurring the corners of the front window. She was a lazy housekeeper. His lips curved in a cynical twist. Why didn't that surprise him?

He pushed the buzzer again, keeping his finger on for a few extra seconds.

He wasn't in the mood to be ignored. Especially by this woman. Impatience rose in a hot, flooding tide. He'd had enough of her ignorant selfishness. Now she would learn just who she was dealing with.

Stepping off the patio, he surveyed the side of the house. Sure enough, one of the windows was wide open, only the flyscreen separating him from the interior. But he'd be damned if he'd resort to illegal entry.

Unless he had to.

Returning to the front door, he pushed his finger down on the bell and kept it there. The incessant peal echoed through the house.

Good! That would shift her. No one could stand that appalling clamour for long.

Nevertheless it was several minutes before he heard the slam of an internal door. And even longer before someone fumbled at the latch.

Anticipation tightened his body. Once they were face to face, she'd do as he wanted. She'd have no choice. He'd cajole if he had to, though considering her behaviour he was sorely tempted to dispense with the niceties and go straight to threats. He'd use whatever tactics necessary. He took a slow breath and summoned his formidable control. He'd need it for this interview.

The door opened to reveal a woman. Obviously not the one he'd come to see but...*sto Diavolo!*

He froze, his composure splintering as sunlight illuminated her features.

His heart slammed against his ribs and sweat beaded his brow. His neck prickled as he stared straight at a ghost.

She had the same classically pure bone structure. The same wide eyes, elegant nose and slender neck.

For a heartbeat, for two, he was caught in the illusion. Then with a single, shuddering breath common sense reasserted itself. This woman was flesh and blood, not a spectre from the past come to haunt him.

Now he saw the subtle differences in her face. Her eyes were a lustrous honey-gold, not dark. Her mouth was a perfect bow, fuller than Fotini's lips had been.

He took in the knotted cloud of her dark hair with its hint of auburn. The creases along her cheek where she'd obviously lain. The crumpled blouse and dark skirt. She must have had an end-of-week celebration last night then crashed out in her work clothes. He took in her pasty colour and the dark rings under her vacant eyes and wondered if it was illicit drugs she favoured or just old-fashioned alcohol.

Did it matter? The sight of her disturbed him, stirring too many memories. But he had no time to concern himself with anyone but the woman he'd raced round the globe to find.

'I'm looking for Christina Liakos,' he said.

She stared up at him, blinking owlishly.

He frowned, wondering if she was sober enough to understand. *'Kyria Liakos?'* he tried in his own language.

Her eyes narrowed and he saw her knuckles whiten on the edge of the door.

'I've come to see Christina Liakos,' he tried again in deliberately slow, precise English. 'Please tell her she has a visitor.'

She opened her lips but no words emerged. Her mouth worked as if she was about to say something, then she shut it and swallowed convulsively. Her eyes were impossibly huge in her face.

'Oh, God!' Her whisper was hoarse, barely audible even from so close. And then in an instant she was gone, stumbling back down the corridor, leaving Costas to stare after her through the open doorway.

He didn't hesitate. A second later he was in the narrow hall, reaching out to pull the door shut behind him.

The young woman lurched into a room towards the back of the house. Her hunched shoulders, the hand clamped over her mouth, told their own story. She'd over-indulged last night and now she faced the consequences.

For a moment he experienced that horrible sense of *déjà vu* once more, sparked by her startling resemblance to Fotini. But he had no sympathy to waste on a stupid young woman who didn't respect her own body.

His senses were on the alert, ready for the confrontation with his quarry. Yet the house had an aura of emptiness. Already he sensed that he and the girl with the hangover were the only ones here. But he had to make sure.

It only took a couple of minutes to check the entire house, it was so small. The place was comfortably furnished and tidy, except for the shambles of a living room, with its litter of bottles, glasses and plates of stale food. And the kitchen, where someone had barely started on the mountain of washing-up.

It must have been some party, he decided, surveying the haphazard stack of platters and the left-over food spoiling on the counter, the glasses jammed into the sink.

And still no sign of the woman he'd come so far to find. The woman who held his future in her hands.

But there was one person who knew exactly where Christina Liakos was.

He turned and strode into the bathroom, only to pull up abruptly.

It wasn't the awful retching sound that stopped him. Or any sense of delicacy at the thought that she might prefer privacy.

To his horror it was the sight of her trim, beautifully rounded bottom in that tight black skirt as she bent over the toilet. And the shapely length of her legs encased in sheer black stockings.

Ridiculous, he told his suddenly alert body. No woman could be sexy while she vomited into a toilet bowl. Even a woman as beautiful as this.

Sophie's eyes streamed as she gulped another breath into her raw, aching throat. Her mouth tasted foul and she shook so hard she could barely support herself. The nausea was fading but her whole skin prickled uncomfortably in reaction. And it felt as if someone had wrapped a band around her head and constricted it till even the throb of her blood hurt.

'Here.'

She opened her eyes to see a damp flannel thrust in front of her. A man's hand held it. A large, square, capable-looking hand with long fingers. Olive skin. A sprinkle of silky dark hair. The sleeve of a finely woven suit. A flash of snowy white cuff. The subdued elegance of a gold cufflink.

Sophie stared but didn't have the strength to reach out.

'I…can't,' she croaked. She felt so weak that it took all her energy to stay on her feet.

There was a burst of sound behind her. Swearing, by the sound of it, but in incomprehensible Greek. And then an arm like hot steel wrapped around her waist and drew her upright till she sagged against the solid wall of his body. His intense heat was like a furnace at her back. But even that couldn't thaw the chill that gripped her.

He swiped the blessedly wet flannel over her brow, down her cheeks, along her mouth and chin and she silently gave thanks to this man, whoever he was.

She recalled looking up into a set face. Into eyes so dark they shone like jet, revealing nothing. Or maybe that illusion was due to the barely leashed anger she'd sensed in him. Even his arrogantly angled black brows lent fierceness to his brooding countenance. He'd had an aura of edginess, of danger, that belied his tailored suavity.

He was a complete stranger. No woman would forget a man like him—all hard, arrogant male and sexy as sin.

Her head lolled against his chest as the lassitude swept her again. She yawned so wide her jaw cracked. As soon as he left she'd go back to bed, she thought dully.

But then his hand was at her shoulder, fingers digging into the tender flesh so that she winced. He shook her and her whole body flopped, unresisting.

'I *said,* what did you take?' His voice was deep, with the hint of an accent, and Sophie felt a tug of feminine response to the timbre of it. 'Tell me!'

Hazily she realised he was speaking to her.

'Tell you what?' Her brain had fogged up. Now the nausea was passing she felt almost human, but everything was so vague.

Only his punishing grip on her shoulder and the way he held her in close round the waist kept her anchored in reality.

His lips were at her ear, his breath hot against her skin as her eyes fluttered shut.

'What have you taken?' His voice was slow and patient but it held a razor-sharp edge. 'Was it drugs? Pills?'

Pills. That was right. She'd taken two pills. Or was it three? She was sure they'd said two only. 'Pills,' she said, nodding. 'Sleeping pills.'

Another burst of cursing. This guy really had a temper problem. She plucked at his arm, trying to free herself. Suddenly she felt trapped rather than supported by his strength.

'Can you stand by yourself?' he asked.

'Of course.' But when he whipped his arm away, Sophie had to grab for the basin to stay upright.

She felt him move away and relief seeped through her weary bones. He'd helped when she needed assistance, but he was a total stranger. As soon as she'd had just a few minutes to gather her strength, she'd make him leave. Her grip on the vanity unit grew desperate as she forced herself to stand straighter.

Was that water running?

She swung round, then wished she hadn't when dizziness swept her. It was a fight to stay standing, even with the vanity unit to lean against.

It was his hands on her clothes that jerked her out of her stupor. The brush of his knuckles as he unbuttoned her blouse. She swatted at his hands but he was too deft. The blouse was already hanging open as he reached round to unzip her skirt.

With a surge of frantic strength she pushed him away with both hands, only to find it wasn't fine wool suiting under her hands, or crisp cotton, but the warm contours of a solid male chest.

What the…?

Dampness hazed his olive skin and his muscles rippled under her hands. She pushed again and felt the tickle of chest hairs against her palms, shooting sensations of pure pleasure through her body. But it was like pushing at a brick wall for all the impact she made. It was an impressive chest.

Right now she was scared, not admiring. Her breath caught on a harsh sob of fear as she tried desperately to thrust him away.

'Leave me alone!' Her voice was breathless, wavering. 'Get out of here now or I'll call the police.'

He ignored her completely, bending instead to tug her pantihose down her legs. His insistent pressure on first one ankle and then the other allowed him to strip it off. If only her coordination hadn't deserted her she might have put up a better resistance.

'I'm not going to hurt you,' he snarled when she aimed a clumsy punch at him and managed to graze his cheek as he straightened. His dark gaze raked her with such disgust that she almost believed him.

She was cradling her fist when he pulled her up and over his shoulder, knocking the breath out of her.

She slumped, disoriented against him, flesh to flesh. The room whirled around her, as dizzying as the blatantly masculine scent of his bare skin. She felt raw heat, rigid bone and muscle, the brush of his hair against her side as he swung her round.

Then, without warning, he slid her down his torso and onto her feet. Straight into a blast of water from the shower. The full force of it hit her back, then her head.

'What…?'

Wet hair streamed down her face, half-blinding her. The pounding water was so heavy it hurt. All that kept her there was the strength of his hands on her shoulders, holding her up and away from him. She swayed and his grip tightened, but he kept her at arm's length.

His dark eyes were unreadable, gleaming with an inner fire. His face was harsh, his jaw set like stone. It was a face Sophie didn't have the energy to deal with right now.

She sagged, her knees loosening, as the water slowly brought her body back to weary, tingling life. Her head fell forward, drooping under the weight of water and of growing consciousness.

This grim-faced stranger thought she needed sobering up, she realised with a fleeting twist of dark amusement. Maybe he thought she'd come close to overdosing. Why else would they both be in the shower in their underwear?

At another time, in another life, she might have thought this scene humorous or embarrassing. Or even provocative. She in white lace bra and panties. The Greek god with the inscrutable eyes and the magnificent body clad in nothing but black briefs.

But not today.

Today was Saturday, she realised, her mind clearing completely as the searing pain of remembrance tore through her chest. No wonder she felt like hell. Yesterday had been the worst day of her life.

'I'm all right now,' she mumbled. 'You can get out.'

Silence.

'I said I'm all right.' She lifted her head and met his stare. If it weren't for the blast of warm water sluicing down she would have shivered at the icy chill of his unwavering gaze.

'You don't look it,' he said brutally. 'You look like you need medical attention. I'll take you to the hospital and they can—'

'What? Pump my stomach?' She blinked at him through the water and wet hair plastering her face. Outrage warred with exhaustion, holding her motionless but for the tremor in her legs. 'Look, I took a couple of sleeping tablets and obviously they didn't agree with me. That's all.'

'How many exactly?'

'Two,' she said. 'Maybe three, I wasn't really concentrating. But not enough to OD, since that's what you're thinking.'

'And what else did you take with the pills?' His voice was sharp, accusing.

'Nothing. I don't do drugs.' Sophie shrugged against his hold and this time he released her. But he didn't move away, just stood there, arms akimbo, blocking the exit. He looked solid, strong, all taut muscle and unyielding bone. His expression was even harder. It made her shudder.

She swayed without him to prop her up. She could still feel

the imprint of his large hands on her upper arms and guessed she'd have bruises there later.

She counted to ten, then, when she managed to dredge up some strength, she turned and twisted the taps closed.

In the sudden silence she could hear his breathing. And the thunder of her own pulse in her ears.

'I didn't have anything else,' she repeated. 'No drugs, no alcohol. This is just a reaction to the pills.'

And to the unrelenting stress of the past weeks.

Slowly she turned back to face him. He looked about as understanding as Ares, god of war, with his flinty gaze and his wide, battle-ready stance.

'I'm sorry you were worried,' she said as she pulled her hair back from her face and looked past his shoulder at the steamy mirror. Anything to avoid staring at the vast expanse of taut masculine skin that scented the damp air with its hot, musky aroma. 'I appreciate your help, really. But I'm OK.' Or as OK as she was likely to be for a long, long time.

For a moment she thought he didn't believe her. Those penetrating eyes surveyed her slowly, clinically and comprehensively. If she'd been capable of feeling embarrassment she'd have shrivelled under that look.

But right now she was strangely detached, felt little except the welling ache deep inside.

At last he nodded tersely and stepped out of the shower. Immediately she sagged, relief slackening her exhausted muscles. He crossed to the cupboard and dragged out a couple of clean towels.

Dumbly Sophie watched him, her brain processing the series of images. The arrogant jut of his uncompromising jaw. His broad shoulders and sleek back: all gleaming-wet, toned muscle. The taut curve of his backside in briefs that clung now like a second skin. Heavy, powerful thighs.

She shivered and dragged in an unsteady breath.

He turned, scooped up his gear and thrust a towel at her. 'I'll get changed in another room.' His deep voice was devoid of emotion.

Was there anything soft about this man?

She watched him stride out the door. No, she decided. He was all adamantine hardness. From the steely strength of his body to his brooding face and cold eyes.

Sure, he had enough humanity to help her when he thought she needed it. Had gone to great lengths, in fact. But not because of kindness, or fellow feeling, she knew instinctively. He'd simply believed it necessary. He'd done what he thought had to be done—kept her conscious before calling medical aid.

She trembled, still holding the towel against her chest. The tremor grew to a shudder and, despite her flushed skin and the steamy fug of the bathroom, that bone-deep chill invaded her body once more.

Sophie stumbled out of the shower cubicle, wrapped the towel around her body and another round her hair, and escaped to her bedroom. Ten minutes later, dressed in old jeans and a comfortable, loose shirt, she went in search of the stranger who'd invaded her house.

Costas stood in the kitchen, sipping strong black coffee. Something to restore normality after his encounter with the girl who looked so much like Fotini.

At first the similarity had been stunning. Even now it was remarkable, despite the obvious differences. This girl was slightly built, more slender. Her face was less round and her cheekbones more pronounced.

He stared blindly into the back yard and swallowed another mouthful of searing liquid. He barely registered the heat. Instead he concentrated on the images that played alternately in his mind. First the sight of her opening the door, so like Fotini that he'd simply gawped in shock.

And second, the picture of her slumped in his hands. Water streaming down, accentuating her seductive curves. His mouth dried as he remembered the narrowness of her waist, the sensuous flare of her hips. Her lacy bra and briefs had been saturated. They had left nothing to his imagination, not the upward tilt of her breasts nor the invitation of her nipples, revealed by the delicate fabric. Nor the evocative shadow of feminine secrecy between her legs.

He'd held her in his hands and immediately he'd wanted her, desired her with a raw, aching hunger that told him he'd been far too long without a woman. Just the feel of her supple, smooth skin against his and he'd known an overwhelming compulsion to have her naked beneath him.

He'd stood there, oblivious to the drenching spray, and wished the circumstances completely different, just for an hour, or two. For long enough to lose himself in the sweet temptation of her. To forget his responsibilities and worries in the mindless bliss he knew he could find in her siren's body.

Costas sipped the scalding coffee and tried to ignore the heavy tension in his lower body. His mission was too urgent. No matter how delicious the enticement, he wouldn't be distracted from his purpose.

The sound of a shuffling footstep made him spin round. She stood in the doorway, apparently steady now on her own two feet. She looked about sixteen in those clothes, and with her hair combed down to her shoulders. But her eyes and the purple shadows beneath them belied that illusion.

Costas frowned as his mind superimposed an image of her, almost naked in her sexy, pristine lace underwear. The baggy shirt failed miserably as camouflage. He'd stripped her, touched her bare skin with his hands. The experience was printed indelibly on his brain.

'There's coffee,' he said abruptly, gesturing to the steaming mug on the table.

She didn't meet his eyes as she sank into a chair and slowly lifted the mug in both hands.

'Thank you,' she said. Her voice was like water: cool, devoid of colour, slipping away to nothing. He felt a moment's burgeoning curiosity then crushed it.

'I need to see Christina Liakos immediately,' he said yet again, curbing his impatience with iron control. 'How do I contact her?'

'You don't.' This time there was something in her tone. Emotion so strong her voice cracked. 'And her name's not Liakos any more,' she added abruptly. 'It's Paterson.'

Her eyes met his and he endured once again that unwanted, unstoppable sizzle of sexual need.

'Who are you?' she asked.

'My name is Costas Palamidis.' He paused, waiting for her reaction but her face remained blank. 'I have an urgent matter to discuss with Ms Paterson.'

'Palamidis,' she muttered. 'I know that name.' Her brows drew together. But clearly last night's excesses hampered the effort of recollection.

Costas shifted his weight, tired of this nonsense. He was getting nowhere.

'I've just stepped off a plane from Athens. It's imperative that I talk to Ms Paterson immediately.' He refrained from adding that it was a matter of life and death. This was too personal, too private to disclose to strangers.

'Athens?' Her eyes narrowed. 'You were the one on the phone.' He watched her perplexity morph into anger. Her coffee mug thumped onto the table. 'You left messages on the answering machine.'

He nodded. 'Messages that were never returned—'

'You bastard,' she hissed, scrambling to her feet so fast her chair crashed to the floor. 'Now I know who you are! You can leave right now. I want you out of here!'

Costas didn't budge. The girl was clearly unhinged. Her eyes were wild and her fingers curved like talons against the edge of the table.

But she was his one lead in locating Christina Liakos. And he'd deal with the devil himself to reach that woman. Deliberately he leaned back against the kitchen bench, crossing one foot over the other.

'I'm not going anywhere. I've come to talk to Christina Liakos or Paterson as she is now. And I'm not leaving until I do.'

Fascinated, he watched the emotions race across her face. Her snarling frown blanked out into staring shock. Then her features seemed to crumple into a mask of pain. She laughed, an ugly, hysterical sound that filled him with a sense of foreboding.

'Well, unless you're clairvoyant you'll have a long wait, Mr Palamidis. I buried my mother yesterday.'

CHAPTER TWO

THROUGH THE SEARING glaze of unshed tears, Sophie glared up at him.

Hell! If she'd known who he was when she opened the front door she'd have slammed it in his good-looking face.

How dared he show up here the day after her mother's funeral and make himself at home? She stared at the mug he held and wanted to smash it right out of his hand. There'd be satisfaction in a violent outburst. She imagined vividly the splash of hot coffee on his snowy white shirt, the look of outrage on his face.

Pity it took all her strength just to stay upright.

Furiously she blinked. She wouldn't let him see her cry. Her grief was too raw, too overwhelming to share, let alone with a man as coldly unfeeling as he was.

She wanted to shout. To rage. Damn it, she wanted to pummel him with her fists till he felt just a fraction of the pain that was ripping her apart.

But what good would that do? Her mother was gone. Nothing would bring her back.

Sophie drew a shuddering breath and lifted her eyes to meet those of her unwanted visitor. His black gaze wasn't quite so unreadable now. Maybe it was the way his eyes had widened, brows raised in surprise.

No, not surprise. Shock. He looked as if he'd just got the shock of his life. In fact, he looked ill—his face suddenly drawn and his complexion paler. A muscle in his hard-set jaw worked, pumping frenetically. It was the only sign of animation in him. He didn't even blink.

Over the sound of her pulse thundering in her ears, Sophie caught the hiss of his indrawn breath. His chest expanded mightily as if his lungs had emptied and he'd only just remembered to breathe.

Then she saw a flicker of emotion in his eyes. Something so fierce that she almost backed away.

'I'm sorry,' he said at last. 'If I'd known…' Again Sophie saw that shadow of turbulent emotion in his gaze and trembled at the force of it. 'If I'd known,' he continued, 'I would not have intruded on you today.'

'You wouldn't have been welcome at any time,' she said bluntly.

He had a nerve, offering her condolences, now when it didn't matter. It was too little and far, far too late.

'Pardon?' His wide brow pleated in a frown just as if he hadn't understood exactly what she'd said.

'I don't want your apologies,' she said. 'I don't want anything from you.'

'I understand that you are grieving. I—'

'You understand *nothing,*' she snarled. 'You with your superior air and your apologies. You make me sick.' She gulped down a raw breath. 'I want you out of my house and I never want to see you again.'

Silence gathered as he returned her gaze, his brows drawing together in a straight, disapproving line.

'If I could, I would leave now as you wish. But,' the word fell heavily between them, 'I cannot. I come here on a matter of great importance. A family matter.'

'A *family* matter?' Her voice rose and broke. How could he be so callous? 'I have no family.' No siblings. No father. And now her mother…

'Of course you have a family.' He stepped close. So close that his warmth insinuated itself into her chilled body, sending tendrils of heat skirling through her. The invasion of her space was strangely shocking.

But she didn't move away. This was *her* home, *her* territory. No way was she backing down.

'You have a family in Greece.'

She stared into his grim face. A family in Greece. For how many years had she heard that? The stubborn mantra of her mother, a woman who'd had to make her life in a new country, far from home. A woman who had refused to be cowed, even by her own father's rejection.

The irony of it. Sophie's mouth twisted in a lopsided grimace at the unbelievable timing. Her mum had waited a quarter of a century to hear those words confirmed. Now, just days after her death, they were being offered to Sophie like a talisman to keep her safe.

'Stop it!' he barked, his hands closing around her shoulders, digging into her flesh.

Sophie jumped, startled out of the beginnings of hysterical laughter. She felt branded by his touch, contaminated. She shrugged, tried to shove his hands off her. Finally he let her go.

'I have no family,' she repeated, staring into his furious gaze.

'You are upset,' he countered as if explaining away her emotions. 'But you have a grandfather and—'

'How *dare* you?' she snapped. 'How can you have the gall to mention him in this house?' Her heart raced so fast she thought it might burst right out of her ribcage. Again she felt the white-hot rage, that savage need to lash out in fury and smash something.

She'd got through the past few days only by refusing to dwell on what she couldn't change, by telling herself that it didn't matter. It was all over now anyway. Old history. No one, not even the cruel patriarch of the Liakos family, had the ability to hurt her mother any more.

And now this family henchman appeared on the scene and dredged it all up again. All the pain and the lacerated hope. The regret and the smouldering hate.

She trembled. But not with weakness this time.

'Do you think there's any place in my life for a man who completely disowned his daughter?' she hissed. 'Who ignored her year after year? Pretended she didn't exist?'

Sophie's chest ached with the force of her hurt, with the gasping breaths she inhaled. Her hands shook with a palsy of repressed fury.

'Who didn't even have enough compassion to contact her when she was dying?' The accusation echoed between them, ebbing away into a silence thick with challenge and pain.

She stared into a face devoid of all emotion. Yet he couldn't conceal the flicker of surprise in his eyes. So this was news to him. And not welcome news, judging by the way his brows drew together.

'Nevertheless, we *must* talk.' He raised a peremptory hand as she opened her mouth to speak. 'I am not your grandfather's emissary. I don't come on his business, but my own.'

Sophie shook her head, confusion clouding her tired brain. His business? It didn't seem likely. Should she believe him or was this some ploy?

'But your phone calls. They came just a few days after I'd contacted my grandfather. I left a message asking him to call.'

Begging him to ring and speak to her mother.

Sophie steeled herself against the memory of those hopeless days. Of the doctor saying there was nothing more they could do to counter the virulent strain of influenza her mother had contracted. Of how Sophie had swallowed her pride and tracked down a phone number for Petros Liakos, the tyrant who'd disowned his daughter, Sophie's mother.

But still the old man hadn't called.

Sophie felt the hatred, the searing pain flood her once more and cursed this arrogant stranger for making her relive it all.

He spoke, his deep voice cutting across the whirling turmoil of her memories. 'I knew of your mother, but not where she was or how to contact her. I needed to speak with her urgently.'

Something about the tension in him, the harsh lines around his mouth, snared her attention, broke through her impotent rage.

'When you rang Petros Liakos,' he said, 'I was able to get your phone number. I called all this week.'

But Sophie hadn't answered the messages from the Greek

stranger that had filled the answering machine. What was the point, when they'd commenced the very day she'd made the funeral arrangements? It was too late for her mother to forgive her family's neglect. And Sophie had no intention of ever forgetting the way the Liakos family had treated her mother.

The messages had become more imperious, more urgent, but Sophie had trashed them. And taken satisfaction in slamming the phone down the one time the Greek stranger had reached her at home.

Now he was no stranger. She looked up into his impenetrable eyes, felt again his aura of implacable power. A shiver of apprehension feathered down her spine.

He claimed not to be her grandfather's lackey.

'Who are you?' she whispered. 'What do you want?'

Costas stared into the sparking, troubled eyes of the girl before him and wished he could leave her to grieve in peace. She was wound up tighter than a spring.

He'd released his hold on her reluctantly, on his guard in case she lashed out. If there'd been a knife to hand she'd probably have swept it up and plunged it straight into his heart. She'd looked like a Fury, eager for vengeance. But the next moment she was heartbreakingly vulnerable.

He felt her grief as a palpable force, heard it in the savage, scouring breaths she took. He exhaled slowly, schooling his face against the pity he knew she wouldn't want to see.

Not for the first time he wished he'd never become entangled with the Liakos family. They were nothing but trouble. Had always been trouble for him. And for her, this girl with the fine lines of pain dragging her mouth down and etching deep around her eyes.

He thrust his hand through his hair and silently cursed this appalling mess.

But he couldn't walk away. He had no choice but to continue. Even though it meant forcing his problems onto a distraught girl.

A pang of guilt pierced his chest. He should give her time. Respect her need to mourn.

But time was the one luxury he didn't possess.

She was right to be cautious, Costas decided grimly as tension hummed through him. This situation had never been simple. And now, since he'd met her, it had become even more complex. Dangerous.

He needed this woman. She was his only hope of diverting the monstrous disaster that loomed ever closer.

But now, to his horror, there was more.

He could barely believe it, didn't want to believe it. It should be impossible. But he couldn't ignore the sheer potency of his physical craving for her. *Of all women!*

It was unique. Inappropriate. It was a complication he didn't need. He didn't have time for lust. Especially not for a grief-stricken girl who saw him as some sort of ogre.

Especially not for a girl from the house of Liakos.

He'd learned that particular lesson long ago.

Look at her! She wore paint-smeared jeans and a baggy shirt. Her trainers were stained and worn and her hair had probably never seen a stylist's scissors.

Yet he couldn't drag his ravenous gaze from her. The elegance of her delicate bone structure stole his breath. Her wide-as-innocence honey-gold eyes, her ripe mouth. Beneath the cotton of her shirt he could see her proud, high breasts. Hell! He could almost feel them against his palms, firm and round and tempting. And those ancient jeans clung to her like a second skin, showing off long, slender legs.

He couldn't believe it. Where was his honour? His respect for her grief?

His sense of self-preservation?

'Who are you?' she whispered again and he saw a spark of fear in her expression.

'My name is Costas Vassilis Palamidis,' he said quickly, spreading his hands in an open gesture. 'I live in Crete. I am a respectable businessman.' In other circumstances he'd have found the novelty amusing, being forced to present his credentials. But there was nothing humorous here.

'I need to speak with you. Is there somewhere else we can talk?' He looked around the room, realising that the untidy remains must be from a large post-funeral gathering.

Damn. It was brutal, forcing this on her now, so soon after her loss. But what choice did he have? There was no time for compassion if it meant delay.

'Outside perhaps?' He gestured towards the back yard. Anywhere away from the claustrophobic atmosphere of mourning that pervaded the house.

She looked at him with wary eyes, clearly unconvinced.

'It's been a long journey and some fresh air would be welcome,' he urged. 'It will take a little time to explain.'

Eventually she nodded slowly. 'There's a park just around the corner. We'll go there.'

She looked so fragile he doubted she'd make it to the front door, let alone down the street. 'Surely that's too far. We could—'

'You were the one who wanted to talk, Mr Palamidis. This is your chance. Take it or leave it.'

Her chin notched up belligerently and faint colour washed her cheeks. Animation, or temper, suited this passionate woman. It was a pity that, given the circumstances, he would not be exploring a more personal acquaintance with her.

Finally he nodded. If she collapsed and he had to carry her back, then so be it.

'Of course, Ms Paterson. That will suit admirably.'

Five minutes later Sophie settled back on the weathered park bench and stifled a groan. He'd been right. She should have stayed at home rather than pretend to an energy she didn't have.

But at least here they were in a public place. And the crisp autumn air felt good in her lungs.

The thought of staying in the house, where this man's presence dominated the very atmosphere, had been unthinkable. It wasn't just his size. It was the way he unsettled her. The indefinable sense of authority that emanated from him. And made her want to put as much distance between them as possible.

Surreptitiously she shot a glance at her companion as he stood a few metres away, answering a call on his phone. From the top of his black-as-night hair to the tips of his glossy, handmade shoes, he was the epitome of discreet wealth, she now realised.

He turned his head abruptly and met her eyes. Instantly heat licked across her cheeks. Yet she read nothing in his expression, not a shred of emotion. His face might have been carved from living rock, a study in masculine power and strength with that commanding blade of a nose and those arrogant eyebrows.

So why had her pulse begun to race?

'My apologies, Ms Paterson,' he said as he snapped the phone shut and sat down. 'It was a call I had to take.'

Sophie nodded, wondering why she should feel so uncomfortable with him sitting almost a metre away.

'My name's Sophie,' she said quickly to cover her nervousness. 'I prefer that to Ms Paterson.'

He inclined his head. 'And, as you know, I am Costas.'

'You haven't really answered me. Who are you?' His height wasn't typical of the Greek men she'd known. And his aura of brooding mastery, of carefully leashed force, set him apart. His features were severe, harsh, but more than handsome. He was unique, would stand out in any crowd.

Why was he here? Her life, and her mother's since settling in Australia, had been ordinary with a capital O.

'Did you know your mother had a sister?' he countered.

'Yes. She and my mum were twins.'

'Your aunt had one daughter, Fotini.' Something in his tone made her watch him intently. His lips had compressed tautly, curved down at the corners. His eyes were bleak.

'A few years ago Fotini and I married, which makes us, you and I, related by marriage.'

'Cousins-in-law,' she whispered, wondering why she found the expression on his face so disturbing. She'd never seen this man anything but controlled. Yet something about his set jaw and the desolation in his eyes told her he clamped down hard on the strongest of emotions.

'Your wife, Fotini, is she here with you in Sydney?'

'My wife died in a car smash last year.'

Now she understood the expression of repressed pain on his face. He was still grieving. 'I'm sorry,' she murmured.

Sophie wondered how she'd feel about her own loss in a year's time. Everyone said the pain would be easier to bear later. That the happy memories would one day outweigh the ponderous weight of grief that pinned her down till sometimes she felt she could barely breathe.

She looked at the man beside her. Time didn't seem to have healed his wounds.

'Thank you,' he said stiffly. Then after a moment he added, 'We have a little girl. Eleni.'

She heard the love in his voice as he spoke and watched his features relax. His lips curved into a fleeting, devastating smile. Gone was the granite-hard expression, the grimly restrained power. Instead, to her shock, Sophie saw a face that was... handsome? No, not that. Nor simply attractive. It was compelling. A face any woman could stare at for hours, imagining all sorts of wonderful, crazily sensual things.

Sophie snagged a short, startled breath and looked away, letting her feet scuff the grass.

'So you do have a family in Greece,' he said. 'There are second cousins. There's little Eleni. And me...'

No! No matter what he said, Sophie would never be able to think of this man as a relative. She frowned. The idea was just too preposterous. Too unsettling.

'And there's your grandfather, Petros Liakos.'

'I don't want to talk about him.'

'Whether you want to discuss him or not, you need to understand,' Costas said.

Sophie refused to meet his gaze and stared instead across the park, watching wrens flit out of a nearby bush.

'Your grandfather isn't well.'

'Is that why you came?' Anger rose, constricting her chest. 'Because the old man's sick and wants his family at long last?'

She shook her head. 'Why should I care about the man who broke my mother's heart with his selfishness? You've come a long way for nothing, Mr Palamidis.'

'Costas,' he said. 'We're family after all, if only by marriage.'

She let the silence grow between them. She didn't trust herself to speak.

'No, I'm not here for that. But your grandfather's condition is serious.' He paused. 'He had a severe stroke. He's in hospital.'

Sophie was surprised to feel a pang of shock at his words. Of…regret. Could it be? Regret for the man who'd turned against her mother all those years ago?

Sophie's lips thinned as she dredged up the ready anger. She wouldn't allow herself to feel anything like pity for him. He didn't deserve it.

'Do you understand?' Costas asked.

'Of course I understand,' she snapped. 'What do you want me to do? Fly to Greece and hold his hand?'

She swung round to face him, all the repressed fury and despair of the last weeks fuelling her passion. 'It's more than he did for my mother. For twenty-five years he pretended she didn't exist. All because she'd had the temerity to marry for love and not in some antiquated arranged marriage! Can you believe it?'

She glared up at him. 'He cut her out of his life completely. Didn't relent with the news that she'd married. Didn't care that he had a grandchild. Was probably disappointed I was only a girl.'

She drew a rasping breath. 'And when she's *dying* he refuses to call and speak to her.' Her voice broke on a rising note and she turned from his piercing gaze, dragging a tissue out of her back pocket and blowing her nose.

'Do you have any idea how much it would have meant to my mother to be reconciled with him? To be forgiven?' She stuffed the tissue away and blinked desperately to clear her vision. 'As if she'd committed some crime.'

'Your grandfather is a traditionalist,' Costas said. 'He believes in the old ways: the absolute authority of the head of the family, the importance of obedient children, the benefits of a marriage approved by both families.'

She looked into his give-nothing-away eyes and his hard face and suspected not much had changed. Costas Palamidis was a man who wore his authority like a badge of identity. Of his blatant masculinity.

'Is that how you married into the Liakos family?' she asked, trying to sound offhand. 'The Palamidis and Liakos clans decided there was benefit in a merger?'

His eyes blazed dark fire and for a moment she felt as if she'd stepped off a cliff without a safety rope. She shivered, for all her bravado, acknowledging an atavistic fear at the idea of rousing this man to angry retaliation.

'The marriage had the blessing of both families,' he said eventually, tonelessly. 'It was not an elopement.'

Which didn't answer her question. Sophie stared into his face and saw the warning signs of a strong man keeping his temper tightly leashed.

That was answer enough. Just looking at him, she knew Costas Palamidis wouldn't settle for anything, especially a wife, unless it was exactly what he desired. He'd get what he wanted every time and be damned to the consequences. The idea of him needing help to get a bride was laughable.

Sophie would bet her cousin, Fotini, had been charming, gorgeous and utterly captivated by her bold, devastatingly masculine husband. No doubt she'd been at his beck and call, deferring to him in everything, like a good, traditional Greek wife was apparently supposed to do.

'Thanks for coming all this way with your news,' she said at last, 'but as you can see I…'

What? Don't care?

No, she couldn't lie. There was a part of her that felt regret at the old man's pain. A sneaking sympathy for him, looking death in the face and deciding, far too late, that he had done the wrong thing by his daughter.

The realisation made her feel like a traitor.

'It's too late to build bridges,' she said quickly. 'I've never been part of the Liakos family and there's no point pretending now that I am.'

She was her own person. Sophie Paterson. Strong, capable, independent. She didn't need some long-lost family in Greece. Instead she had friends, an address book full of them. And she had a career to start, a life to get on with.

Yet right now she wanted nothing more than to lean against this silent stranger and sob her eyes out till some of the pain went away. To let his obvious strength enfold and support her.

What was happening to her?

This weakness would pass. It must, she decided as she bit down hard on her quivering lower lip.

'You've made your feelings abundantly clear.' His deep voice scraped across her raw nerves so she shivered. 'But it's not that simple to disconnect from your family.'

'What do you mean?' She swung round on the seat. For all his calm composure, there was an inner tension about him that screamed its presence. Immediately she shrank back, suddenly aware of how very little she knew about him. Of exactly how much larger and tougher he was.

'Don't look like that,' he growled. 'I don't bite.'

She shivered at the immediate, preposterous idea of him bending that proud head towards her and scraping his strong white teeth over the ultra-sensitive skin at the side of her neck.

Where the heck had that come from?

Her breathing notched up its pace and her heart thudded hard against her ribcage. Sophie whipped round away from him, horrified that he might have registered the flash of awareness still rippling through her.

She squeezed her eyes shut. She was off balance. The funeral, the lack of sleep, were taking their toll.

'Sophia—'

'Sophie,' she corrected automatically. She'd rejected the original version of her name as soon as she was old enough to realise it belonged to the world of that far-away family who'd treated her mother so appallingly.

'Sophie.' He paused and she wondered what was coming next. He sounded as if he had the weight of the world on his shoulders. 'I came to find your mother because it seemed she was the only person left who might be able to help.'

'Why her?'

'Because she's family.' He sighed and from the corner of her eye she saw him thrust his hand back through his immaculate hair.

'My daughter is very ill.' His voice now was brusque to the point of harshness. 'She needs a bone-marrow transplant. I hoped your mother might be a match to donate what Eleni needs.'

The words, so prosaic, so simple, dropped between them with all the finesse of a bomb.

Appalled, Sophie felt the words sink in. She found herself facing him, aware for the first time that some of his formidable reserve must be a product of his need to clamp down on an unbearable mix of anguished emotions.

'You're not compatible yourself?' she asked, then realised the answer was obvious. He wouldn't be here if he'd been able to help his little girl.

But she wasn't prepared for the wave of anger that swept through him. His hands clenched dangerously and his whole body seemed to stiffen. There was no mistaking the expression in his eyes this time. Fury. And pain.

Silently he shook his head.

'And no one in your family—?'

'No one in the Palamidis family is a suitable donor,' he cut across her tentative question. 'Nor are any of your relatives.' He paused, dragging in a deliberate breath that made his chest and shoulders rise.

He must feel so helpless. And there was no doubt in her mind that Costas Palamidis was a man accustomed to controlling his world, not being at its mercy.

Sophie's heart sank as she realised how dire the situation was.

If the girl's own father wasn't a match for her marrow type, how likely was it that she would be?

He might have read her mind. His voice was grim as he continued. 'Nor did we have luck finding a match in the database of potential donors. But your mother and her sister were identical twins. So there's a possibility.'

'You think I might be able to donate bone marrow?'

'That's why I'm here.' He spread his fingers across his thighs, stretching the fine wool of his dark suit. 'Nothing else would have dragged me away from Eleni now.'

Sophie felt the weight of his expectation, his hope, press down on her, even heavier than the burden of grief she already carried. She had a horrible premonition that he was doomed to disappointment.

How desperate he must have been to fly to Australia, not even knowing if her mother was here. And how distraught when she'd hung up on him and deleted his messages. No wonder he'd looked like an avenging angel when he'd stormed the house and demanded to see her mother!

She shivered and wrapped her arms tight round her body as a sense of deep foreboding chilled her.

All his expectations, all his dark, potent energy, had shifted focus. He wanted her.

CHAPTER THREE

COSTAS FORCED HIMSELF into a semblance of patient stillness as the girl beside him digested the news.

Admitting that the chance of success was slim had brought the black fear surging back. The inescapable truth that for all his power and authority, this was one thing he couldn't make go away.

He'd give anything to save his daughter. Do anything. He wouldn't hesitate a second to take the illness into his own body, if only it were possible. Anything to save Eleni.

Instead he'd been forced into a role of unbearable powerlessness. He'd demanded the best medical attention, engaged the top physicians and bullied Eleni's distant relatives into testing their compatibility to donate bone marrow. All to no avail.

If the doctors were to be believed, this girl beside him was the only hope his daughter had left.

It was the smallest of chances. But hope was all they had left, he and Eleni. He'd bargained with God and would tackle the devil, too, if it meant they could overcome this disease.

Why didn't Sophie Paterson say something? Why not answer his unspoken question?

His hands fisted so tight that pain throbbed through them. The muscles of his neck and shoulders stiffened into adamantine hardness as he fought the impulse for action. He wanted to shake her into speech. Bellow out that she was their last hope. She had to take the test. *She had to.*

What was she thinking?

He reviewed the material the private enquiry agency had just phoned in about her and her mother. A pity they hadn't reported before he'd arrived at her house. He winced, remembering his demand to see Christina Liakos.

Sophia Dimitria Paterson was twenty-three, had just finished her course in speech pathology, an only child. Her father had died in an industrial accident when she was five. Her mother had worked as a cleaner to support them.

He wondered how Petros Liakos would feel, learning his once-beloved daughter had spent years working double shifts to keep food on the table. Such a far cry from the pampered life she'd led in Greece.

Sophie had worked as a waitress part-time while she studied. She liked to party. Was outgoing and very popular, especially with young men.

Educated but no money. In fact, according to the financial report he'd just heard, Sophie Paterson had inherited a substantial debt from her mother.

Why didn't she say something, damn it? Wasn't it obvious what he wanted from her?

Or was she waiting for him to persuade her?

He darted a measuring glance her way. Surely not. She didn't seem the type.

But then he had personal experience of exactly how acquisitive and devious women could be. It wasn't a lesson he needed to learn twice.

Unable to contain the urgent need for a physical outlet for his tension, he shot to his feet, towering over her as she stared into space. He shoved his fists into his trouser pockets, hunching his shoulders against the hollowing pain he refused to admit into his consciousness.

For an instant her eyes met his. Then quickly she shifted her gaze.

In that moment Costas felt the last of his hard-won control tear apart. The social niceties, the veneer of the civilised world were stripped away, like a long, uncoiling ribbon, leaving him free of everything but his desperation.

'If it's money you want there's plenty of that to sweeten the choice for you.'

Her head swung round and she stared up at him, eyebrows arched. As if she didn't already know just how wealthy the Liakos family was.

And their riches were nothing compared to his. Would she do what he wanted for money? He'd met too many people, including beautiful young women, who'd sell their integrity, much less some bone marrow, for a tiny fraction of his material wealth. And she was a Liakos. He knew exactly what that family was capable of.

Still, the idea that she could be bought sickened him. He swallowed down hard on the sour taste of disappointment and swung away from her.

'Your grandfather set aside a legacy for Eleni. Money and company shares.' His tone was clipped. Anything to get this over with. They'd strike a bargain and settle it.

He sensed her involuntary movement and knew he had her hooked. He heard her breath catch.

'If the doctors say you're a match and you go through with the procedure,' he continued, 'I'll arrange to have that legacy passed to you instead. There'll be no argument from your grandfather, I'll guarantee it.' He paused, letting her wait for the clincher. 'I haven't had it valued, but I guarantee it totals well into seven figures.'

Silence.

No doubt she was imagining what she could do with several million dollars. Already in debt, she'd be eager to take up the offer.

'Is that all?'

'What?' He swung round. She stood at his shoulder. Colour tinted her cheekbones and washed across her slender neck. Her eyes were brighter too.

Again he experienced that shaft of molten desire straight to his lower body. But now he felt contaminated by it. Even in lust his taste was usually more discriminating. Gold-diggers had never held any appeal for him.

'Is that the last of your offers?' she asked.

He ignored her attempt to bargain for more and cut to the chase. 'You'll agree to be tested and take my terms?'

'I'll agree to nothing, you arrogant bully.'

He stared down, shocked to realise the gleam of avarice in her eyes was instead a flare of blatant fury. No sign here of a grasping, money-hungry opportunist. She looked as if she'd like to tear his eyes out.

Could he have got it wrong?

'You might think you're a big man but you're just a hollow sham.' She shoved her mass of riotous hair back behind her shoulder and squared up to him, toe to toe. Her head barely topped his shoulder. Her chin jutted at an impossible angle as she glared at him.

'What gives you the right to assume that I'm some heartless, avaricious monster?' She jabbed his chest with her index finger. 'Who'd take *money,*' jab, 'to help a sick child?' Jab and twist.

'I bet you didn't put this proposition to any of your relatives back in Greece, did you?'

He opened his mouth to argue. But she was right. They were family. They'd be mortally offended at the very idea. But Sophie Paterson… She was Eleni's family, yet she was an unknown quantity.

He refused to question the way his mind shied from the idea of her being part of *his* family.

'Of course you didn't,' she almost spat at him. 'You wouldn't offend your daughter's *real* family.' Again that jab into his chest. 'But we Australians…we were never up to scratch, were we? You'd expect the worst from us.'

Her voice rose in strident accusation yet he saw the glitter of unshed tears in her eyes. Her soft mouth quivered and she bit down so hard he feared she'd draw blood.

Burning shame seared out from the accusing point of her finger, through his torso, right to his heart. It wasn't an emotion he was used to. And he didn't like the sensation of guilt one iota.

'Enough,' he growled, clamping one hand round hers and pressing her open palm across his shirt.

His heart leapt at the contact, thudding an uncontrollable tattoo, and he fought the impulse to drag her into his arms and stop her voice with his mouth. Her lush lips were open now, in a circle of surprise that made him want to dip his head and discover the taste of her on his tongue. She'd be sweet as honey. Hot as flame. Heat burst across his skin, just at the thought of it.

Anger. Guilt. Lust. They rushed through him in a feverish swirl that escalated into raw desire. So savage it slammed through him with a force that almost made him reel.

He dragged oxygen into his air-starved lungs and stared down at her, wondering. He knew desire—had no trouble assuaging it. But he'd never felt anything like this before. Ever.

What the hell had he got himself into?

Sophie blinked up into his glittering black eyes and felt the blaze of fury that had buoyed her through the outburst dwindle and fade.

He was so close she could see that, for all the severe planes and angles of his face, his skin was fine-grained and smooth but for the rough shadow along his jaw. Her nostrils flared as she detected and instinctively responded to his scent: heat and musk. One hundred per cent pure masculine pheromones.

'Enough,' he said again, his voice a husky growl that sent all her nerves into alert.

For an endless space their eyes met and held, an indefinable heat pulsing through the crackling silence between them. If she could have broken his hold she would have backed away, put some distance between them till she felt safe again. When he looked at her like that she couldn't think. And she didn't want to feel.

'You have my apologies,' he said at last. He shook his head decisively when she would have spoken. 'In the extremity of the situation, I leaped to the wrong conclusion. I saw your silence in the worst light.'

He paused and dragged in a breath so deep that his chest almost touched hers.

'I have experience in dealing with people who are not so…unaffected by material wealth as you.' His eyes, darkly mesmerising, held hers. 'I regret the offence my words caused you.'

His heart drummed beneath Sophie's fingers, the encompassing heat of his body surrounded her. His eyes seemed to gaze right into her soul. If she could have looked away she would. But the intensity of his scrutiny held her in thrall, as surely as if he'd bound her physically to him.

This was dangerous. She had to end it. Now.

'I accept your apology,' she said, wincing at the stilted sound of her voice. 'I was hurt that you believed…' She shook her head. What did it matter now? 'It was a misunderstanding,' she said as graciously as she could.

'Thank you, Sophie.' His voice was a low burr, brushing across her skin.

And then he did something totally unexpected. He lifted her hand, raised it to his lips and, gaze still meshed with hers, pressed a slow kiss to the back of it.

A jolt of sensation speared through her and her eyes widened. For a moment she saw the reflection of her own shock in his ink-dark eyes, and then they turned blank, giving nothing away. But ripples of awareness raced through her body, awakening dormant senses into stirring life.

It scared her.

She tugged her hand away, rubbing it with her other thumb, as if that would erase the burning sensation of his mouth on her flesh. He stepped back and she released the breath she hadn't known she'd been holding.

For the first time she looked, really looked, at Costas Palamidis. Trying to see beyond the stereotype she'd assigned to him.

He was more than the epitome of ruthless machismo she'd first thought him. More than a father fighting against the odds for his daughter's life. He was clearly used to dealing with wealth and power, and from what he'd said, with the sort of people she'd prefer to avoid.

The grimness of his face had seemed bone-deep when they'd

met. But was it simply the overlay of despair on a man protecting his family against the worst possible odds?

And there was more to ponder over. Now she'd seen that spark of undiluted sexual energy in him, felt its potency in her own crazily jangling nerves. It set off every alarm bell in her brain. But she couldn't simply walk away from him. Not now she understood why he was here.

She was no closer to understanding who Costas Palamidis was. And, she realised, she was torn between wanting to have nothing more to do with him and the disturbing need to find out everything.

Sophie drew in a slow breath, acknowledging that she was in deep trouble.

Something had happened in that short, violent storm of emotions. Some barrier had been breached, some internal barricade splintered, leaving her feeling wide open and defenceless. She hadn't a clue how, but now, instead of feeling only grief at her loss and fury at the thought of her grandfather, a new mix of feelings swirled within her. They threatened the iron-hard control that had kept her going through the last few weeks.

Something about this man, this stranger, had reached straight out to her, unsettling her in ways she didn't comprehend.

He wasn't her type. Not at all. Big, bossy, take-charge guys weren't her style. So how could she explain this feeling of linkage, of a bond between them?

She couldn't.

'Now we understand each other.' His voice was low, vibrant, making her aware of her body's immediate response of shimmering excitement. Just to the sound of him!

She nodded, not trusting her own voice.

'And you'll help?' There was unmistakable urgency in his controlled tone.

'Of course I'll do what I can,' she said. 'I couldn't ignore your little girl.'

His smile was taut, perfunctory. Already he was planning his next move; she could see it in his eyes, in his ready-for-anything stance. He was probably deciding how best to manage the logistics of the test.

'But don't forget,' she warned, reaching out a hand as if to restrain him, then losing her nerve and letting her arm drop to her side, 'there's no guarantee it will work.'

His look told her what he thought of her caution. 'It's got to work. There's no other option.'

He made it sound simple. As if the outcome were assured. Sophie shivered. The bleak reality was that she probably wouldn't be able to help his daughter.

But she didn't voice her caution again. She understood too well the desperation of watching a loved one wither away before your eyes. The eagerness with which you snatched any hope, no matter how tenuous. The constant prayers, the belief that somehow you might *will* them to survive.

She'd been like that as her mother lay in hospital, unable to fight the disease that robbed her of life far too early. And it was like that now with Costas Palamidis.

He might look hard as nails. In fact, she was sure he *was*. But the weary lines fanning from his eyes, the carved lines bracketing his mouth, revealed a pain that was no less real for being savagely hidden behind his formidable reserve.

That must be why she felt this unique connection to him. As if there was far more between them than their status as cousins-in-law.

Sophie breathed a deep sigh of relief. That was it. Of course there was a rational explanation. Fellow feeling for someone suffering the trauma she'd been through.

She looked up into his severe face and told herself it would be all right. She didn't need to worry any more about the inexplicable fusion of awareness and fear that he evoked in her. It had an explanation after all.

Steadfastly she ignored the trickle of unease that slid down her spine as her eyes met his. Fire sparked again deep within her.

'I'll make all the arrangements,' he was saying, and for the first time his gaze was warm with approval.

The trickle disappeared as a wave of heat washed over her.

She nodded, trying to concentrate on what lay ahead and ignore her physical response to that look.

'Can you be ready tomorrow?' he asked.

'Sure.' The sooner the better.

'Good.' He took her elbow and turned towards her house, pulling her along with him. His hand was hot through the sleeve of her shirt and his warmth at her side enfolded her. Her chest constricted strangely, as if all the air had been sucked from her lungs.

'I'll organise our flight for tomorrow,' he said.

Sophie faltered to a stop. 'Sorry?'

'Our flight.' He sent her an impatient glance and started walking again, guiding her beside him. 'I'll call you with the details and drive you to the airport.'

'I don't understand.' She frowned. 'It's just a medical test, isn't it? A blood test or something?'

'That's right,' he said. 'A blood test, and if that's compatible the doctor will take a bone-marrow sample.'

'Wait!' She planted her feet wide on the ground so this time he was forced to stop and face her. 'What's this about a flight?' she demanded. 'Surely the tests can be done in Sydney?'

His dark brows arrowed down in a V. 'They can be done anywhere. But this way you'll be on hand if the doctors say we can go ahead with the transplant.'

Again Sophie felt that stab of unease at his presumption this would work. That she would be Eleni's donor. But what if the news wasn't good?

'You're taking a lot for granted. It would be easier if I come to Greece once we know if this will work.' That would be time enough for her to face her mother's relatives. The very idea of that made her stomach churn.

His hand curled tighter round her elbow and he drew her up against his body. She stared into his face, so implacable, so determined that for a single, startled moment Sophie's breath stopped.

Out of nowhere surfaced the mind-numbing idea that he wasn't going to release her. Ever.

* * *

Costas stared down into her dark-honey eyes and told himself to slow down, to be patient. And, above all, to ignore the searing realisation of just how good it felt to touch her. To feel her body against his.

She was grieving.

She was off-limits for all sorts of reasons.

But she felt so right, tucked here against him. Her fresh scent had teased him from the moment he'd pulled her close, awakening long-dormant senses. Old needs.

He wanted…

Carefully Costas released his hold and stepped away, putting some space between them. Her chest rose and fell with her choppy breathing and he could see the reflection of his own puzzled response in her face.

No. This wasn't about what he wanted from her. That could never be. This was about what Eleni *needed* from her. Nothing else could be allowed to cloud the issue. Nothing.

He stepped back another fraction and let his hands drop to his sides.

'It will be simpler and faster this way,' he said. He refused to voice the superstitious fear that if he let Sophie out of his sight, left Australia without her, this opportunity to save Eleni might slip through his fingers. That something would prevent Sophie from coming to Greece. He clenched his hands together behind his back.

'I could go to a clinic here in Sydney—'

'We can be in Athens in a day,' he interrupted. 'And when I ring ahead the doctors will be waiting for you. You can have the first blood test the next day.' He held her gaze with his, willing her to agree. Then he forced himself to spell out what he'd left unsaid before. 'This is my daughter's last chance.'

The words echoed between them, appalling, unbearable.

His body was tense with the effort of control, aching with the stress of it. He broke eye contact and stared into the distance, not seeing the unfamiliar Australian scene, or the slim woman before him. Remembering instead his little Eleni, so brave and uncomplaining. So innocent. What had she done to deserve this?

Couldn't Sophie understand his need to get this done *now?* As soon as humanly possible?

He flinched when she touched him, so unexpected was it. And so shockingly familiar to his hungry senses.

He looked into her upturned face. The sympathy he saw there would have broken a lesser man. Her eyes were huge in her pale face and she stared at him as if she understood just how desperate he was.

In all these nightmare months there'd been no one to share the anger and the fear, the horror of fighting the temptation of despair. He hadn't realised till this moment just what a difference that would have made.

And now here was this girl offering him sympathy and understanding. And all the while her body spoke to his, tempting with its heady promise of ultimate physical release.

For an instant he teetered on the brink of reaching out and grasping what she offered. But he didn't need anyone. He'd learned to stand alone long ago.

'I understand,' she said, the knowledge of his pain there in her husky tone. 'And I promise if I'm compatible then I'll be on the first plane to Athens.'

'No!'

That wasn't good enough. He'd exhausted every other avenue. He couldn't afford to let her stay behind. A thousand things could happen, even in a few weeks, to prevent her trip to Greece.

'No,' he said again, striving for a normal tone. 'You'll come now. I'll make the arrangements. And if,' he forced himself to go on, 'you're incompatible, you'll have lost nothing by it. You won't be out of pocket. You'll be my guest, of course.'

He watched her open her mouth as if to protest, and then close it again.

'A short break from here won't hurt. You haven't any pressing engagements, have you?' He knew from the investigator she had nothing, neither study nor work, scheduled.

Slowly she shook her head.

His spirits rose as he scented victory. 'Look on it as a short holiday,' he said, using the low, coaxing tones that always got him what he wanted with women.

She met his gaze and he felt something deep inside stir, unsettling him again. She was just a young woman, like so many others he'd known. Why did he have the gut-deep sensation that she saw into his very soul?

Sto Diavolo! Maybe the strain was starting to tell on him after all.

'I'll pay my own way,' she responded, her soft mouth setting in a mulish line that brought back a flood of memories when he least expected it.

Practice helped him to curb his temper and persuade instead of order. 'You'll be visiting Greece to help my daughter. It will be my pleasure to have you stay with us.'

The girl had such pride! He knew she couldn't even afford the airfare to Athens, would have to organise a loan for the trip.

'It's not Liakos money,' he added. 'You would not be obligated to your grandfather.'

For another long moment her gaze locked with his. Then she nodded once. 'All right. I'll come to Greece. And I'll pray the tests turn out the way you hope.'

There was deep sadness in her voice. Her eyes were shadowed and he guessed she was remembering her mother. How she'd been unable to save her.

He reached out and took Sophie's elbow. He moved slowly, his touch on her arm light, knowing how much she must be hurting. She'd never guess the sudden violent surge of adrenaline that shot through him at her words. The immediate, searing lightness that flared in the recesses of his mind.

This was going to work.

They were going to save Eleni.

CHAPTER FOUR

SOPHIE STEPPED THROUGH the airport's sliding doors.

She was here, in Crete.

She took a deep breath, wondering how the air in Greece could be just the same as home, but somehow different enough to send a quiver of emotion through her. She bit her lip. She wasn't going to cry, was she?

It wasn't as if this place meant *anything* to her.

But it had meant so much to her mum. Despite the painful memories, her mother had been an optimist. She'd planned to bring Sophie here. A girls' trip, she'd said, badgering Sophie into organising a passport in anticipation of the day when they'd have money saved to travel. And if they weren't able to visit family, there were lots of other things to see in Crete.

Sophie blinked rapidly against the bright light. She'd planned to surprise her mum and buy their tickets after she'd been working professionally for a year.

It would never happen now.

Nearby people milled and talked, called out greetings and embraced each other. Welcomes and departures.

And Sophie had never felt so alone in her life.

'Are you all right?' A hand touched her elbow, guided her forward.

A *frisson* of awareness snaked through her at the sound of that deep voice, the fleeting warmth of his hand. She sucked in a breath and schooled her features into what she hoped was a bland expression.

Costas hadn't touched her since their conversation in the park back in Sydney. He'd been scrupulous in keeping his distance. And she'd convinced herself she'd imagined her response to him.

But this was frighteningly real. Instantaneous. Devastating.

'I'm OK,' she said, scanning the bustle of activity, rather than turning to look up at him. 'Maybe a little tired.'

'You can rest when we reach the house.' He dropped his hand and Sophie felt as if a constricting weight lifted off her chest, allowing her to breathe freely again.

'We'll soon be on our way. And it's not too far along the coast to my home.' He gestured to a limousine parked straight ahead. It was long, dark and gleaming.

She should have expected no less. Obviously she'd stepped into another world: one of wealth and privilege. There had been the assiduously helpful airline staff, the VIP treatment through Customs and the discovery that, far from spending the long flight to Athens with hundreds of other economy travellers, Costas had obtained the whole first-class cabin for them alone.

That had astounded her. But anything was possible to the man who owned the airline, she'd discovered.

Had this been the world her mother had given up for love? No wonder Petros Liakos had been shocked at her choice of a penniless Australian for her husband.

Sophie walked slowly towards the limousine, suddenly dreading the idea of what awaited her at the end of this journey. How would she ever live up to Costas Palamidis' expectations? What if she couldn't help?

But she hadn't been able to refuse him.

She'd almost been convinced that if she didn't leave Sydney willingly, he'd scoop her up into his arms and bring her here by force. The grim, absolute determination in his face, in his battle-ready stance, in his piercing dark eyes, had spoken of a man who stood outside the civilised conventions of polite request and negotiation. He'd looked as if he welcomed any excuse for action. As if he was prepared to bundle her over his shoulder and smuggle her away to his private lair in Greece.

The fantastical notion still sent a shiver of appalled excitement through her.

But what had decided her to come was the vulnerability she could only guess at, hidden behind his obstinate determination and aura of aggressive, macho power. She'd caught a glimpse of it in his eyes when he'd spoken of Eleni. She knew it was there, deep inside him. The love for his daughter, the fear for her. Sophie could relate to it far too well.

'Here we are.' Costas gestured her towards the rear door of the vehicle. A young man in uniform stood smiling, holding it open for her.

The discreet buzz of a phone sounded and Costas stopped, frowning at the number displayed. 'Excuse me a moment,' he said. 'It's a call from the house. I'd better take it.'

Sophie sensed the immediate tension in him as he stepped aside, saw the grimness around his mouth as he lifted the phone to his ear. He was expecting bad news.

Sophie paused, couldn't help but watch. Just how bad could the news be?

Then she saw his lips curve up in a smile. His tender expression stole her breath away. 'Eleni,' he said. And what she heard in his voice made her turn back to the car and the waiting driver, feeling like a voyeur. It didn't matter that the conversation was in rapid Greek, too quick for her to follow. It was far too personal for her to intrude.

Costas stared up at the vivid blue bowl of the open sky, heard his little girl's chatter in his ear and thanked the lord he was home again at last.

And with such excellent news! The hope he'd been searching for so frantically.

He listened to Eleni's story of the kittens she'd seen just yesterday, and of how useful a cat would be, to keep the nonexistent mice at bay. He almost laughed aloud at her transparent tactics.

There was a grin on his face as he promised once more that he'd be home soon and said goodbye. He swung around towards the car, eager to be on his way.

There was Sophie, the embodiment of their last hope. He quickened his step. She wasn't in the car, but stood, talking to Yiorgos. The driver had lost some of his professional aloofness and was standing close, gesticulating as he spoke. As Costas watched, Sophie smiled, then started to laugh, a light sound that teased at his senses.

He paused, watching the play of expression across her face. The shadows of grief lifted from her face and he saw her as she must have been before her mother's illness. Carefree, happy… stunningly beautiful. Her vibrant loveliness tugged at him, stirred deep-buried feelings into life.

Yiorgos said something and Sophie laughed again, her eyes smiling appreciatively at her companion. Costas' breath hissed between his teeth as a stab of sensation speared into his chest.

Discomfort. Annoyance.

Jealousy?

No. That wasn't possible. He barely knew the woman. Had no claim over her. No interest in a personal relationship. The idea was ludicrous.

He shoved the cellphone into his pocket and strode over to the car. 'Ready?' His voice was brusque.

Yiorgos immediately snapped to attention and into position beside the door. Sophie's smile faded and she looked away.

Costas felt disappointment percolate through his elation at being home.

What more did he want? He had what he'd sought: the chance to save Eleni. That was all that mattered. There was nothing else he needed. Not this woman's smiles nor her company.

This persistent awareness, his physical response to her, was damned unsettling. Especially to a man like him, who relied on no one but himself. Who had learned to doubt rather than to trust. To be cautious rather than impulsive.

He waited for Sophie to settle herself into the car, then sat in the far corner of the wide back seat.

Avoiding her gaze, he began explaining their surroundings, giving her a tourist's guide to Heraklion. Detailed, informative and totally impersonal.

It reinforced his role as host and helped him erect the barriers that weakened whenever he looked at her. Barriers that were essential if he was to get through the next few days.

Sophie leaned back in her corner of the seat and listened to Costas describe the bustle of Heraklion harbour and some of the city's history and traditions. He really did love the place.

But despite his enthusiasm for his home town, she sensed a change in him. The man beside her didn't meet her eyes. He spoke with the clipped, precise tones of a professional guide.

Had she done something to offend him?

Not that she could think of. Despite her long sleep on the plane she was probably jet-lagged, imagining things. And after all, wasn't this distant Costas Palamidis easier to cope with than the man she'd faced in Sydney? With his raw passion that both scared and fascinated her? She'd felt almost powerless against the force of his personality and his dark emotions.

She told herself she was glad of the change in him.

They drew up before a sprawling, modern house twenty minutes later. A house unlike any Sophie had ever seen, let alone entered. One glance confirmed what she'd already discovered: this man had more money than she'd ever dreamed of.

As the car pulled to a halt in the turning circle, the large front doors opened and a woman stepped out. A tall, grey-haired woman, holding a small child in her arms.

Costas flung open his door and was out of the car as it stopped. Sophie watched through the tinted glass as Costas strode across the gravel, arms open to take the tiny child in his arms. She must only be about three or four, Sophie decided, her heart wrenching as she took in the little girl's pallor and her bald head, evidence of her medical treatment.

A lump the size of Sydney Harbour settled in her throat and she blinked back tears. *Oh, lord, let it be all right. Let me be able to help her.*

Her own door opened and she looked up into the smiling face of Yiorgos, the chauffeur.

Now or never.

Sophie took a deep breath and swung her legs out of the car, registering but ignoring the sudden onset of exhaustion as she stood up. It had been a long trip. And now she felt every kilometre of it: the weariness of travel and the burden of expectation. She walked slowly towards the house, unwilling to interrupt the family reunion.

There was a trill of laughter from the little girl in response to Costas' deep murmur. Then he turned and Sophie stopped dead, anchored to the spot by the change in him.

The shadows had fled from his face. There was love in his eyes as he hugged his daughter, a softness about his mouth. He looked younger, sexier, more vibrantly alive. A grin a mile wide transformed him from the brooding man she'd known into someone new. Someone who had the power to knock her off balance even at a distance of ten metres.

Then, as Eleni moved in his arms, Sophie's gaze turned to her, taking in her tiny, fragile form and her huge dark eyes, so much like her father's.

The little girl stared at her for a long moment. Then she wriggled in Costas' embrace and held out her arms towards Sophie.

Clearly, unmistakably, she called, *'Mamá.'*

CHAPTER FIVE

GRATEFULLY SOPHIE SIPPED the scalding coffee. It was too sweet for her taste, but it was just what she needed. The coffee traced a welcome trail of heat that counteracted the deep chill of shock still gripping her.

She listened to the retreating sound of high heels tapping across the polished floor in the foyer. To the soft stream of rapid-fire Greek as Costas' mother spoke to her son on her way out.

For the first time in years Sophie wished her language skills were better. She'd rebelled early, refusing to attend Greek classes as soon as she was old enough to understand the rift between her mother and her family in Greece. But now she'd have given a lot to understand what Mrs Palamidis said to her son. And more to know what his murmured responses were. Even from here, the sound of his deep voice made her stomach muscles clench in awareness.

Mrs Palamidis had been so welcoming. So understanding and sympathetic, apologising for the shock of Eleni's words, ushering Sophie in here to the elegant sitting room to recuperate while Costas went to settle his daughter for an overdue nap.

But now she'd left and Sophie would be alone with Costas. And later, with little Eleni.

That moment when Eleni had looked at her with such excitement and called her *Mamá*...

Sophie shuddered. She'd been horrified. She felt as if she'd stepped straight into her dead cousin's shoes. Her stunned gaze had turned from the little girl to Costas and she saw in his face a flash of emotion so strong and tortured that she knew without doubt he was remembering his wife. And the knowledge had been like a knife twisting in her breast.

Why hadn't he told her that there was a family resemblance between her and her cousin? Had he been afraid she wouldn't agree to come to Greece?

She couldn't escape it, could she? Everything came back to family. Costas' driven determination to save his daughter. The precious DNA linking Sophie to Eleni. The uncanny physical similarity to a dead woman she'd never met. The bond that bridged half a world and still couldn't be denied, despite the high-handed rejection by her grandfather.

No wonder the very air had seemed alive with tension and old remembrances when she'd stepped out of the airport.

Sophie's eyes filled with burning tears as she thought of her mother. How much she'd have loved to reconnect to the family she'd left behind.

Her mum would have taken it for granted that Sophie would take the first plane to Greece in the circumstances. She wouldn't have thought twice about the pain of reopening old family wounds if it meant helping a child.

Inevitably Sophie thought of her grandfather, recovering from his stroke somewhere on this very island. But her sympathy didn't extend that far. The man who'd disowned her mother could be on another planet as far as she was concerned.

A shadow of movement at the far end of the massive sitting room caught Sophie's eye and she looked up. There, filling the doorway with his broad shoulders, stood Costas. She couldn't read the expression in his eyes at this distance, but there was a watchful quality about his stance that made the hairs on the back of her neck stand up.

She shivered and straightened in her seat. 'Your mother has left?'

'That's right,' he said, and the timbre of his deep voice was like the brush of fine sandpaper across Sophie's nerves, stirring life and awareness where before there was chilled numbness. 'My parents live several kilometres away.'

So they were alone. She and Costas Palamidis. Why did the idea send a skitter of anxiety through her?

He strode across the room to stand near the end of the sofa where Sophie sat. He seemed to invade her personal space and she had to make a conscious effort not to tuck her feet back away from his.

She knew from the glint in his eyes that he recognised her discomfort. There was a slightly mocking arch to his black brows as he returned her look. Then he frowned and settled himself on the long leather sofa opposite her.

'I apologise,' he said, 'that your arrival should be so…difficult. If I'd guessed how Eleni would react to the sight of you I would have warned my mother, asked her to explain to Eleni before you arrived.'

His expression was deeply brooding, his regret obviously genuine. And she felt her indignation drain away, despite the appalling situation he'd put her in.

The joy that had lit his face as he'd held his daughter in his arms was a faded memory. Back instead was the dour stranger burdened by care.

It disturbed Sophie to realise how much she wanted another glimpse of that other Costas.

'It's all right,' she murmured. 'There's no harm done. It was just a surprise.'

'More than that, I'm sure. You looked white as a sheet when Eleni called out to you. I should have—'

'It's over,' she interrupted, then paused as a horrible thought penetrated her weary brain. 'You *did* explain to her, didn't you? She doesn't think—?'

'No. I explained that your resemblance to her mother is because you are cousins. Eleni understands now that you are a very special visitor, who has travelled around the world to see her. She was so excited I'm surprised she went to sleep. She can't wait to play with her long-lost cousin.'

'But surely—' Sophie began.

'You're not scared of spending a little time with her, are you?' he challenged, his frown deepening. 'She's only a child, and a very lonely one. She hasn't been able to mix with other children as she normally would, because of her treatment. And now, for obvious reasons, she's curious about you. Is it too much to ask?'

'I was just going to say that I may not be here long, so it might be better not to interfere with her routine.'

But it was more than that, Sophie admitted to herself. There was something that made her want to hold back from this family, from Eleni and her father. Perhaps the superstitious desire not to tempt fate by believing she really could help the child, despite the odds. Or maybe it was a primitive fear of taking a dead woman's place, even if only for a short time. And that instantly made her think of Costas, not Eleni.

She shot him a glance under her lashes and found him watching her intently. There it was again. That sense of compelling force, drawing her towards him, as if she had no will of her own when he was around. It scared the living daylights out of her, this awareness, this attraction. And she wasn't ready to cope with it.

'I'm sure a little change in routine won't harm Eleni in the least. We must make the most of you while you're here with us.'

Sophie's breath jammed in her chest as his gaze dropped to her lips, lingering there for a moment too long before flicking back to her eyes. It felt as if her ribs were constricting in against her, making it hard to breathe. Her heart drummed to an increasing tempo that echoed in her ears.

The room seemed full of the heavy awareness strung like a tangible weight between them.

Sophie leaned forward abruptly and put her cup on the coffee table between them with a click. Her hand was trembling. And the way he looked at her only exacerbated the tremor. She shot to her feet.

'You have a magnificent home,' she said, determined to steer the conversation to a subject that was simple and impersonal. Something to break the uneasy connection building between them.

'I'm glad you approve, Sophie.' Even his voice was different:

a rich, caressing burr that vibrated through her, drew her skin tight and shivery.

Late-afternoon sunlight slanted through the huge panoramic windows, highlighting what she could have sworn was a trace of grim amusement on his features. Surely not. There was no way he could guess at the unholy mix of trepidation and excitement she felt, knowing she was alone with him.

She spun on her foot and walked towards the enormous curving line of full-length glass that comprised one wall. She guessed it was an expensive, architectural masterpiece. But she barely registered it. Her mind was fully occupied with the man she felt watching her.

'I've never seen anything like it,' she said at last, cursing the way her voice emerged: light and breathless. 'It's so modern, so unique, yet somehow it fits its surroundings.'

Brilliant, Sophie. I bet he really wanted that incisive commentary on his home. The place had probably featured in prestigious architectural digests.

'A friend designed it,' he answered. 'Someone I went to school with. He knows me and what I wanted so that made the job simpler.'

Below her stretched a silver-green vista: an ancient olive grove surrounded by a dry packed stone wall, sloping down towards the sea. Beyond it glinted the dark water of a cove, enclosed on two sides by headlands. It was peaceful. Enticing.

She guessed the place had looked like this for hundreds of years. Possibly thousands. And there was no other sign of habitation in sight. But then if you had Costas Palamidis' fortune you wouldn't want to share this slice of paradise with neighbours.

'That's a big sigh.' His voice came from just behind her and she froze. 'Are you sure you're all right?'

'Yes.' She made herself turn towards him, but didn't meet his gaze. 'I'm just tired.'

'Of course. It's been a long journey. If you come with me I'll show you your room.'

There was nothing in his voice now to alarm her. Nothing at

all. His tone was bland, as if the searing look he'd sent her before had been the product of her imagination.

Sophie chanced a peep at his face. It was set in the harsh lines of control she recognised from their first encounter. He looked as hard as flint and just as unfeeling.

The speed of his change from feverish intensity to chilly reserve threw her completely off balance. She would never be comfortable with this man.

The silence as they made their way through the luxurious reception rooms was almost oppressive. Taut with the strain of undercurrents that set her nerves on edge. Tinged with the unsettling awareness that they were alone except for the child sleeping upstairs.

'Why didn't you tell me I looked like my cousin?' she blurted out as they ascended a sweeping marble staircase.

It was a relief to break the humming silence.

His wide shoulders shrugged beside her, but he continued up the steps without breaking his stride. 'It wasn't important.'

Not important? Sophie stopped, clutching the banister with one hand. Not important that she looked enough like his dead wife to convince the woman's own daughter?

Ahead of her he halted, turned and looked down at her. His eyes had that awful blank look she remembered from their first meeting. As if he was clamping down on every vestige of emotion.

'I should have told you. But, as I explained, it didn't occur to me that Eleni would react as she did. I can only apologise again.'

Sophie read his tightly compressed lips, the rigid tilt of his jaw, and suddenly wondered how *he'd* reacted when he'd first seen her. Had he immediately thought of his dead wife?

He must have, of course. And perhaps that accounted for some of his searing anger that first day. To be confronted by someone who so closely resembled the woman he'd loved and lost must have been a terrible shock.

'It's all right,' she lied. Eleni's reaction had rocked her. She released her stiff fingers from the metal railing and started forward again.

She reached the stair where he waited for her with his unreadable eyes, his closed expression.

'Are we so alike, then? Fotini and I?'

There was no mistaking the flare of emotion in his eyes at her question. The spasm of quickly controlled movement through his big body.

Perhaps she shouldn't have asked, should have respected his obvious grief for his wife. But she had to know.

His night-dark eyes held hers as he shook his head. 'No,' he said brusquely. 'At first glance there's a superficial similarity, but the differences are much stronger.'

Oddly, instead of reassuring her, the knowledge that she was unique, not a mirror image of Fotini, didn't comfort as it should have. Or perhaps it was the dismissive way he brushed aside the resemblance. She supposed in his eyes no one could compare to the woman he'd loved.

Sophie drew a slow breath and started up the stairs beside him. What did she want? For him to look at her and see his wife? For him to respond to her as he had to Fotini? As if she were the woman he loved?

No! Of course not.

'I hadn't realised Eleni would remember what her mother looked like so well,' she said. 'But then I don't know much about small children. If it's been a year since—'

'Ten months,' he said as they reached the top of the stairs. 'Ten months almost exactly since the accident.'

Sophie cursed her tongue as she heard the pent up anger, the fierce emotion in his tone. She wanted to reach out to him and…

And what? Soothe his pain?

Who was she to ease another's grief? She could barely contain her own. Couldn't begin to understand what it would be like to lose a spouse, a partner you thought would be yours for life.

'Eleni has a photo of her mother in her room,' he said, interrupting her thoughts. 'I put it there when Fotini died. It seemed to help Eleni when she missed her mother.'

Sophie wondered if photos had helped Costas deal with his

own loss. Looking at the rigid set of his shoulders, she thought not. He was obviously a man still very much in love with his wife.

'Here we are,' he said briskly, standing aside and gesturing to a pair of doors. 'This is your suite. Your bags have been unpacked for you.' His smile was perfunctory as he added, 'I'll leave you to rest and settle in.'

He turned then and walked away, his whole frame rigid. With disapproval or pain?

Sophie wondered why it mattered so much to her. Why she wanted to run after him and try to comfort him.

Just as well she had too much sense for that.

The rest of the evening passed in a blur that Sophie hoped was due to jet lag. By the time she'd showered and changed and eaten the meal Costas insisted she have on a tray in her room, she was exhausted.

A maid bustled out, wishing her a good night. And Sophie even managed to laugh at her earlier sense of claustrophobia, at the idea of being alone here with Costas. She hadn't been thinking clearly enough to realise that a house this size must have a full-time staff on the premises.

Her room alone would have swallowed up at least half of her home in Sydney. And the bathroom! A cleaner's nightmare with all that gleaming marble and the massive mirrors on two walls.

She shrugged into her old cotton wrap and padded across the thick carpet to the glass doors. Just one more look at that magnificent view and then she'd sleep. She stepped outside into the darkness, letting her eyes adjust to the silvery light of a half moon and the jewelled panoply of stars. They were away from the city here and it was quiet. So quiet she could hear the soft shushing of the waves in the cove.

Sophie drew a deep breath of fresh night air, registering the unfamiliar scents. Salt of course, from the sea, but something else too. Herbs? It smelt like oregano and thyme, rosemary and something else, spicy and sweet.

She approached the corner of the long curving balcony, only

to pull up abruptly as a darker shadow detached itself from the gloom and blocked her way.

'Can't you sleep, Sophie?' His voice slid like heavy silk against her skin, right down her spine. And heat flared in the secret, feminine core of her.

Costas thrust his hands deep into his pockets, feeling them curl into tight fists as he caught her delicate scent on the night breeze.

He'd come out here to think, to gather the tatters of his control in preparation for another day of desperate hope and unspeakable fear. He'd begun to find solace in the still darkness.

And then she'd appeared, ripping at the shreds of his self-possession like a blade.

It was torture being so close to such temptation. Craving the numbing, mindless ecstasy that he knew he could find in her body. Yet knowing he couldn't afford to act on his primitive instinct to take, to hold, to tame.

She was off-limits for all sorts of reasons. Not least that she was his guest. He had a duty to protect her, even from himself.

'I just thought I'd get a breath of fresh air,' she explained, her voice so high and light he knew with a deep, visceral certainty that she felt it too, this force that drew them inexorably together.

She half turned, as if to leave, and the light behind her silhouetted the luscious upthrust curve of her breasts.

His indrawn breath hissed between his clenched teeth and her head swung round.

For a frozen instant neither moved, his galloping pulse the only animation. Then he forced himself to speak. 'Don't leave on my account.' His throat was raw with the effort of control, making his voice a grumbling murmur. 'I was just going in.'

In the darkness he felt her eyes on him. It was a touch that heated his skin to fever pitch.

'No! Don't go. I didn't mean to intrude on your privacy.' She sounded breathless, distressed.

His mother's warning this afternoon came back to him again. *She could be so easily hurt, Costa. Treat her well.*

Caution didn't come easily to him. But he wasn't reckless enough to give in to this beckoning temptation and cross the demarcation line that kept them apart. Anyone could see that disaster lay that way. For both of them.

'It's all right, Sophie. I was going in to check on Eleni anyway.'

He forced himself to move forward, passed her so close that her body heat warmed his side. Her enticing fragrance filled his nostrils and his fists clenched so tight that they throbbed. Tension gripped his neck and shoulders in a vice.

He kept his eyes fixed on the door to Eleni's room further along the balcony and made himself keep walking. 'Enjoy the peace for a little longer. Then get a good night's sleep.'

She'd need it for tomorrow.

Yes, that was what he needed to concentrate on—the blood test, the options for Eleni's treatment. The long discussion he'd have with the medics tomorrow. Anything but Sophie's lithe body, warm and inviting, just metres away.

'Goodnight.' Her voice was a light whisper that made him falter. Then he hunched his shoulders and strode on.

CHAPTER SIX

IT WAS LATE IN THE MORNING when Sophie woke and her head felt thick and heavy. She'd slept through the night but disturbing dreams had plagued her. Fortunately for her peace of mind, she couldn't remember them. But she suspected they'd featured a pair of probing black eyes.

She ate her solitary breakfast in a sunny parlour while another maid explained that the *kyrios,* the master, was busy conferring with his daughter's doctor. Her meal finished, Sophie took the opportunity to explore.

The French windows on this side of the house led to a wide flagged terrace, then down to an immaculate lawn. She strolled across it, feeling the warmth of the sun on her face, hearing the unfamiliar birdsong and, in the distance, a dog barking. There were scents here too, from the border of bright flowers that edged the lawn, from fruit blossom somewhere near, and inevitably from the waves that she could just hear rolling in to shore in gentle rhythm.

Sophie closed her eyes and breathed it in. The sounds and warmth and smell of the place.

A sense of peace settled on her. Perhaps because she was so far from home and her real life. From the pain and drudgery of the everyday. She felt that, just for now, she could relax and enjoy the moment.

A gurgle of laughter caught her attention and her eyes

snapped open. There, rounding a path at the end of the garden, was Eleni, pedalling unsteadily on a bright orange tricycle. Behind her followed a young woman, close enough to ensure she kept her balance.

Sophie watched as, inevitably, Eleni looked up and saw her. She didn't understand it, but she felt almost guilty. As if she shouldn't be here, strong and healthy, when such a tiny child was battling the odds for survival. As if somehow it would be *her* fault if the transplant couldn't take place.

But it was too late to slink away.

The laughter died away as Eleni saw her, her eyes widening. She stopped pedalling and planted her feet on either side of the tricycle.

Her face was grave as she said, *'Kalimera sas.'* Good morning to you.

'Kalimera, Eleni.'

Immediately the little girl's eyes brightened and she tilted her head to one side as if to get a better view of her new cousin. Then she launched into a hurried spate of Greek that Sophie had no hope of following.

'Siga, parakalo,' Sophie said, smiling. Slow, please. *'Then katalaveno.'* I don't understand.

Eleni's mouth rounded in astonishment and the girl with her bent to explain that Sophie didn't understand Greek.

'I speak a little,' Sophie said. 'But it's been a long time since I used it.' They'd spoken English at home.

'Unfortunately Eleni doesn't speak English,' said the girl, who introduced herself as Eleni's nanny.

But the language barrier didn't deter Eleni. She climbed off her trike and headed straight over to Sophie, barely pausing before she reached up for her hand.

Sophie felt the tiny, warm fingers close round hers. She looked down at Eleni's pale, serious face, at her dark eyes, old beyond their years, and something, a hard, cold knot deep inside her, shifted suddenly and began to thaw.

No wonder Costas had been so adamant that she come to Greece. Life was too precious to waste. And, looking down into that pinched little face, Sophie had an inkling of the protective love he must feel for his daughter. The desperation to find a way to save her.

'Ela,' said Eleni insistently, pulling her hand. Come.

Out in the garden, he'd been told. But where? Costas scanned the pool, the lawn and all the areas closest to the house. As long as Sophie hadn't decided to go for a long walk along the shore. The doctor was waiting inside, ready to take her blood sample for the initial compatibility test.

Costas strode past the formal gardens and headed for the path that led through fruit trees to the olive grove and then to the beach.

The doctor would wait, that wasn't a problem. But he, Costas, wanted it done *now*. He had to know what chance there was for this to work.

He had to—

His head shot up as he heard laughter, lilting and evocative, ahead. His steps slowed as he rounded a hedge. And then he stopped.

Bright sunlight illuminated two heads, one bare and pale, the other dark, with a thick mane of hair that gleamed with the tiniest, seductive hint of auburn.

Eleni and Sophie. Cross-legged in the grass of the old orchard, bending over something in the meadow grass.

'Beetle,' said Eleni in Greek.

'Beetle,' said Sophie.

'Green beetle.'

'Green beetle,' mimicked Sophie.

His daughter was teaching Sophie Greek. Behind them, on the stone wall, sat her nanny, making a daisy chain.

'Nose.' Eleni placed her finger on Sophie's nose.

'Nose.' Sophie copied the gesture and then gave Eleni's button nose a tiny tweak, making Eleni giggle.

Costas swallowed down hard on the lump that rose in his throat. He'd heard his little girl laugh so rarely in recent months. It was the best sound he'd heard in ages.

He must have moved then. Something made the pair of them

look up. Immediately Eleni clambered to her feet and raced across to wrap her arms around his legs. *'Papa!'*

He'd never grow tired of her embraces. Even if, the good lord willing, she grew to be a mother herself.

He bent down and swung her up high in his arms and around till she squealed with delight. Then he tucked her close against his torso, inhaling her sweet, fresh soap scent. Felt her tiny, warm body wriggling against his.

And over her shoulder his eyes locked with Sophie's. The laughter had faded from hers and now he saw there the welling emotion he battled so often himself.

A shaft of heat pierced his chest, warming places that had been frozen against the pain. The knowledge of her understanding did that to him. It promised so much.

But it also threatened his control.

'Come,' he said, turning abruptly away. 'There's someone to see you.'

Costas stood on the front steps, watching the doctor's car disappear down the driveway. The warmth of the sun was on his face, the light sea breeze tickled his collar. He registered the physical sensations but that was all.

He didn't feel anything else. Not excitement, not the fervent hope of yesterday. Not even the impatient anticipation he'd expected.

His emotions had shut down.

Or was he lying to himself? Pretending he didn't feel anything so he wouldn't have to face the yawning chasm of fear that might suck him down if he let it? Fear that the test result would be negative.

'Costas?' The voice was soft, tentative.

He'd never heard his name on her lips, he realised. And he liked it. Liked it too much for a man whose emotions were supposed to have shut down.

'Costas, is everything all right?' Closer now, Sophie's voice came from just beside him. Her hand settled on his sleeve, feather-light, tentative, and immediately fire sparked in his bloodstream. He clenched his fists to prevent his instinctive response: to cover her hand with his own and keep it there.

He turned to find her looking up at him. The sun caught the highlights in her hair, illuminated the purity of her classically beautiful features. But they were nothing to the impact of her gold-flecked eyes. She returned his gaze openly, with such candour and sympathy, that he felt the warmth of her compassion like a caress.

How had he ever, even for an instant, thought she looked like Fotini's mirror image? There was no comparison between the two.

Fotini had been so alive, so full of passion, but there'd been precious little generosity in her. She'd been too wrapped up in herself. She'd been vivacious, but never, not once, had she connected with him the way Sophie did with just this single, heartfelt look.

A shudder rippled up his spine, a presentiment of destiny drawing close.

No! He didn't believe in such things.

Sophie didn't understand him. How could she? He barely understood his own feelings. There *was* no connection.

He thrust away the desire to lean down and draw whatever comfort he could from her. She tempted him to forget how fickle women could be. However sweet the illusion, experience had taught him well.

Yet it disconcerted him to realise how much he wished the illusion were real.

'Yes, everything is fine,' he said, surprised to find his voice had dropped to a gravelly murmur. He stepped back, felt her hand fall, and knew it was better that way.

'The doctor said he'd ring as soon as he could with the results,' she said. 'It won't be a long wait.'

Costas experienced a sudden, futile wish that the results might be delayed. What would he do if the news was bad? If a transplant wasn't possible? How would he face Eleni? The thought of it scared him as nothing else had.

He needed to get away, do something to fill the next few hours, he suddenly decided. Waiting here for news would drive him crazy.

'It's almost time for Eleni's lunch,' he found himself saying. 'Then she has a long nap. Would you like to do a little sightseeing? Or are you too tired from the journey?

He watched her intently, waiting for her response.

He *wanted* to spend time with this girl, he acknowledged. Despite the way she got under his skin, challenging his composure and his expectations. Despite the turmoil, the confusion he experienced whenever they were together, something about her drew him every time. And it wasn't just sex.

Maybe, if he got to know her, he could work out what it was—that indefinable something that set her apart from other women he'd known.

'Thanks,' she was saying, not quite meeting his eyes. 'I'd like that. If you've got the time.'

'Of course.' He'd already put in several hours' intensive work this morning on the phone and the email. An afternoon off wouldn't hurt. 'It will be my pleasure.'

An hour later he strode out of the house. Eleni was tucked up in bed, asleep after a story on his lap. He'd postponed his afternoon teleconference and he was eager to get away.

Just a sightseeing drive, he told himself. Simple, uncomplicated. A host's duty. But that didn't prevent the sizzle of anticipation he experienced as he remembered Sophie's warm gaze meshing with his. The subtle temptation of her body when she stood close.

He slid on his sunglasses and turned towards the garages. Strange that Yiorgos didn't have the limousine waiting at the front door as instructed.

Her voice alerted him first. Automatically his step quickened. Sure enough, there she was, deep in conversation with his driver. The pair had their heads together over a map spread on the bonnet of the limo. Yiorgos was tracing a finger along some route, all the while leaning closer than necessary towards the woman at his side.

But Sophie didn't mind. She was laughing, flicking her hair

back over her shoulder in a gesture obviously designed to encourage the driver's attention.

Déjà vu.

It slammed into him with nauseating brutality.

In the shadows of the garage it could have been Fotini standing there, flirting. That siren's smile, the provocative angle of her head, the ripple of laughter. The two women were so alike in that moment.

Fotini had never done more than flirt with anyone else after their marriage—he'd made sure of that. But when the mood was upon her she'd found a perverse delight in flaunting herself with other men, teasing Costas with the sight of her sharing an emotional intimacy she denied him.

A cloud blocked the sun and Costas registered a sudden chill in the sea breeze.

Yiorgos said something and Sophie leaned forward, peering over the map. The movement stretched her jeans taut, emphasising feminine curves in a way that made the muscles in Costas' belly spasm tight and his throat dry. His hands itched to reach for her.

Silently he cursed himself for his inevitable reaction. And for being so disappointed in her. Hadn't he told himself she was no different?

'Ready to go?' His tone was carefully even, revealing none of his simmering anger.

Yiorgos jumped, clear evidence of a guilty conscience, and put a decent distance between himself and Sophie.

She swung round, a tentative smile on her lips. The look of welcome on her face made it seem as if she'd been filling in time, waiting for Costas' arrival. Unbidden, answering warmth flared in his belly.

But he wasn't fooled by her.

'Not the limo today, I think.' He gestured curtly to one of the other vehicles. 'We'll take the Jaguar. No need for you to drive us,' he said over his shoulder to Yiorgos.

Minutes later they were heading along the coast road, Costas describing the local highlights. That should have distracted him from the unreasoning disappointment that had taken hold when he'd seen her amusing herself with Yiorgos.

Why was he surprised? It must be second nature to her, as it had been to Fotini, to seek male attention. Hadn't the investigator's report specifically mentioned Sophie's popularity with the opposite sex?

The knowledge should make it easier for him to resist the temptation she represented. After all, he had discriminating tastes. He didn't share his women.

Yet still he burned for her. And that made him furious.

'You do not mind driving alone with me?' Costas asked. 'I should have asked if you'd prefer the limousine.'

'No, this is lovely. It's a beautiful car.' Sophie smoothed her hand over the seat—she'd never felt leather so soft.

'I'm glad you like it.' Costas' deep voice thrummed across her skin, drawing it tight. She looked up and for a moment met his eyes, dark and glowing with an intense emotion she couldn't identify. Then he turned his attention back to the road and she let out a slow breath, wondering how he managed to affect her so with just a glance.

'Some women prefer not to be alone with a man who is not a close friend or family member.'

Sophie frowned at the edge in his voice. He was showing her the local sights—what was there to object to in that? 'In Australia no one would think anything of it.'

She turned and stared at the coastal development they were approaching. It was modern and brand-new. But her attention was caught by the figure of an old, black-clad woman, leading a laden donkey down a narrow lane right beside the massive new structures.

'I suppose the customs here are different from those at home,' she murmured.

'Things have changed, but some of the old ways linger. We still have a strong tradition of protecting our women.'

Her mouth pursed at the idea. Much good it would have done her or her mother to wait for their male relatives to protect them! 'In Australia we're independent. Women look after themselves.' It came out as a challenge. But then he'd hit a raw nerve. Far from looking after his womenfolk, Petros Liakos had shunned them, left them utterly alone to sink or swim. If that was an example of Greek male protectiveness she wanted nothing to do with it.

Her mother had made her own way, against the odds, in a new country. Sophie remembered how exhausted her mum had used to be after her long shifts and how that never stopped her putting in a few more hours, taking in ironing for extra money. Never once had she complained.

'You never felt the need for protection? Not even from unwanted male attention?'

Why the sudden interest? He wasn't thinking of setting himself up as some sort of male guardian, was he? Instantly she rejected the disturbing idea.

'I find there's safety in numbers.' It was much better having a large group of friends.

He sent a piercing stare her way. 'So, you have many male friends? Doesn't that make life complicated?'

She frowned. 'Not at all. Sticking with one guy isn't all it's made out to be.' Her one serious boyfriend had turned out to be a disappointment. And after that experience Sophie wasn't eager to rush into intimacy again.

Now she found it easier to be part of a group. There was no pressure to pair off and she could go out and enjoy herself without worrying about sexual politics. Simpler. Safer.

Sophie felt Costas' scrutiny and turned to meet his brooding look. His expression had settled into grim lines that accentuated the stern set of his face.

His disapproval was obvious.

So, he didn't think women should take charge of their lives? She tilted her chin and looked out at the view, surprised at her disappointment.

For a while there she'd felt as if she and Costas were developing a tentative understanding. She was dismayed to discover how strongly she felt his rejection.

Why should it matter so much to her?

CHAPTER SEVEN

SOPHIE LEANED BACK against the trunk of an old pine tree and felt her body relax, muscle by muscle. It was so peaceful here, so quiet. She didn't ever want to move.

Only Costas' presence, so temptingly close, marred her contentment. He was silent, absorbed in his own dark thoughts, staring up at the snow-covered peaks where Mt Ida caught the clouds.

He couldn't see how hungrily she followed the crisp line of his profile against the sky. The angle of his jaw, the curve of his lips, the lean strength of his broad shoulders.

If only he'd…what? Turn and talk to her? Share his thoughts?

Or look at her again the way he sometimes did—so that her blood seemed to thicken in her arteries, beating slower and harder as excitement dried her mouth.

She needed to get a grip, cultivate some distance from the man. That was what common sense told her. But if she was honest with herself she'd admit common sense had little to do with the growing feelings she had for Costas Palamidis.

She'd seen him battling fear and despair. His elation when that first test had shown positive and she'd gone to hospital for a bone-marrow sample. The demons of doubt that rode him now, days later, as he waited for news. She'd seen him so heartbreakingly gentle with Eleni and couldn't help wishing he'd share some of that tenderness with her.

She had no business wanting more from a man who'd recently lost his wife. But she did.

These past days in Crete Sophie had let herself be lulled into hoping something…meaningful was developing between her and Costas.

Each afternoon, while Eleni slept, she and Costas drove out, exploring the countryside. These trips were a source of secret anticipation and intense disappointment. Sometimes she felt as if she and Costas connected in a way she never had with anyone. There was a warmth of shared understanding, a spark of something special between them, that made her blood sing and the shadows fall away. And then, in the next instant, it disappeared. She could feel his withdrawal.

Did she imagine their growing understanding? Sometimes she'd swear it was real. And others…

The one constant was the undeniable thread of simmering attraction that bound them. Even when Costas' expression was dark, almost disapproving, the magnetism drew them, like polar opposites, together.

He threatened her peace in ways no man ever had. Her mind turned to mush if ever his suddenly hot gaze trawled over her face, or he drew so close she could inhale his scent. Awareness, expectation, excitement were a constant throb in her blood whenever he was near.

Nothing had prepared her for it. Her one intimate relationship hadn't been even a poor reflection of these intense feelings.

How she wished her mother were here to advise her. To share her experience and wisdom. But Sophie was on her own.

Abruptly she turned away. Perhaps if she stared at the ruins spread out before her she could imagine it as a thriving city. Anything to take her mind off Costas and this see-saw of emotions.

But ancient Phaestos stubbornly remained a confusion of stone foundations. Not nearly as fascinating as the man beside her.

'Have you thought any more about your grandfather?' he asked so suddenly that she jumped. She felt her eyes widen as she swung round to meet his gaze.

Of course she'd thought about him. How could she not when she knew he was so close, on this very island? She nodded.

'But you're not willing to let the feud go?'

'It was *his* feud, not mine!' She felt the familiar, instant surge of hot fury. 'It was up to him to end it.' Her chest rose and fell with angry breathing. 'And I did *try*, remember? I rang him and never got a response.'

She read sympathy in his expression and something else. Something that made the hairs rise on her nape. 'Why do you ask?'

'I think perhaps he does want to end it.'

'What do you mean?' Her eyes narrowed suspiciously.

'I've heard something that may change your views.' He paused. 'According to his housekeeper, Petros Liakos intended to call your mother.'

A jolt of something—shock? Disbelief?—slammed into her.

'You mean that's what he says now?' So he'd changed his tune now it was he who lay in a solitary sick bed.

Costas' expression grew severe. 'No. He hasn't spoken about it. When the housekeeper told him of your call, he asked her to bring the letter from your mother. Apparently when she first wrote he instructed his staff that any mail from her should be set aside and not delivered to him.'

'Unfeeling bastard,' Sophie murmured, her heart clenching at the memories of her mother enclosing a photo with the letter she wrote to Petros Liakos each year on her daughter's name day.

'The point is,' Costas' words broke across the painful recollections, 'he hadn't realised she'd written again. Apparently he was shocked to discover how many letters there were.'

Sophie said nothing. She refused to have any sympathy for the old man.

'The housekeeper left him in his study.' Costas paused. 'When she returned later he'd collapsed across the desk. There were letters and photos spilled onto the floor and his arm was stretched out towards the telephone.'

Sophie could see the image so vividly she couldn't see

anything else for a moment. Not the bright sky, nor even the man so close beside her.

'You think the news precipitated his stroke?' Nausea swirled in the pit of her stomach, rose like a tide, engulfing her.

'I've no idea,' he said. 'But I felt you should know.'

'I… Thank you.' Sophie shook her head, trying to clear the whirling thoughts that bombarded her. If her grandfather *had* been trying to call, how tragic that he hadn't succeeded. For her mother and for him.

Sophie shot to her feet and took a few faltering steps away, breathing deeply to counter the shock of this news. For it *was* a shock. It didn't change the essentials—her grandfather was obviously an arrogant, domineering old man, too proud for his own good. But still…

'You would prefer I hadn't told you?' Costas' voice had a rough edge that sent a tremor of reaction racing across her skin.

'No. You did the right thing.' Sophie stared out over the stones of the old city, her vision blurred, her throat closing. She wrapped her arms round herself, trying to hold in the pain of conflicting emotions. Grief for her mother was a constant. But now it melded into something more complex and confusing.

'But the pain is still raw,' he murmured. 'Almost too much to bear.' The words came from just behind her, feathering the tender skin of her neck. She spun round, automatically stepping back so that he stood at arm's length. Even so his dark gaze mesmerised her, filling her vision.

The yearning for his touch, for the comfort of his embrace, was almost overpowering. She had to force herself to stand rigidly still, not stumble closer as she so desperately wanted to do.

'You are strong, Sophie. Stronger than you think. Eventually, one day, the hurt will ease.'

She looked up into his sombre face, letting his words wash over her. It was his expression that held her attention, the fierce concentration on his proud features as he watched her.

She felt the tension between them spike, the still afternoon air was thick with it. His gaze had never been so unfathomable or more tantalising.

'Whatever your grandfather's mistakes, they are in the past, they're behind you.' he said.

But it wasn't that simple. It seemed she had unfinished business with Petros Liakos.

And now, here, right this minute, she *had* to find out if she was imagining the unnerving intimacy between herself and Costas. The need to know was a driving force that overwhelmed caution.

Were his words simply trite encouragement from an acquaintance? Or did he feel what she felt—a strengthening bond of understanding between them?

She took a single step, closing the gap so that the heat of his body encompassed hers. She shivered, feeling as if she'd stepped into danger. Her nostrils flared as she recognised the warm scent of his skin. It sent a jolt of desire right through her. She tilted her head up towards his. Her heartbeat raced as she saw his mouth just a whisper of breath away from hers.

Anticipation hummed through her, her body swayed infinitesimally closer. She *willed* him to reach for her, to tell her he'd felt it too—the sense of rightness when they were together.

That was what she wanted—wasn't it? To put an end to this suspense? She'd imagined his embrace so often these last days, the need for it had consumed her, keeping her awake well into the long nights.

Yet still he stood, looking down at her, neither encouraging nor discouraging. His lips had parted slightly as if ready for the taste of her. Excitement twisted ever tighter in her belly, urging her on. She could kiss him if she just reached up and pressed her mouth against his.

He expected it too: the gleam in his eyes told her that, as did the throbbing pulse at the base of his neck.

But he wouldn't take the initiative. Sophie understood that with sudden, devastating clarity that halted her instinctive move towards him.

Why? Why wait for her to make the first move? He must read the invitation in her eyes.

She hesitated on the brink of committing herself.

And then the answer came to her, like a bolt out of the clear sky, stabbing straight to her heart.

A shadow stood between them, a shade of the past. Costas looked at her but, she realised, he didn't see her, not really. He was attracted to her because she reminded him of the woman he'd loved and lost just ten months ago. Her cousin, Fotini.

Sophie stumbled back a pace, horrified at what she'd almost done. The acrid taste of disappointment filled her mouth.

'What is it?' He took a step forward and she raised her hand to stop him. The soft linen of his shirt grazed her palm and she dropped her hand as if it burned. She couldn't touch him. Not now.

'It's Fotini, isn't it?' she whispered. 'You look at me like that because you're thinking of her.'

Costas met her stunned, hurt gaze and felt as if the ground had opened up beneath his feet. If it weren't for the pain in Sophie's eyes, the hurt in her trembling lips, he might have laughed at the absurd idea.

His body *ached* with the effort of repressing his desire for her. He'd struggled not to follow his instinct and kiss her senseless as he'd wanted to ever since she'd sat down on that bed of pine needles.

Vivid images of him and Sophie, together on that soft carpet, had kept him fully occupied. So much so that he hadn't been able to look at her—had turned instead to stare out into the distance. But the scent of her, the whisper-soft echo of her breath, the knowledge of her being *there,* so close to him, had tested his self-control beyond all reasonable limits.

Him pining for Fotini! For the woman who'd destroyed his belief in the possibility of marriage as a partnership. Who'd viewed their wedding simply as a stepping stone to more wealth she could squander. Who'd cruelly rejected her own daughter and taught him a bone-deep distrust of women. Beautiful women in particular.

He grimaced. He supposed he owed Fotini some thanks. She'd stripped the scales from his eyes. It was that experience alone that kept him sane in the face of the temptation Sophie offered.

He knew Sophie was no Fotini. Few women could be that self-absorbed and destructive. But since his marriage he understood that what he felt for Sophie was best dealt with in a bedroom: no strings attached.

Even so some part of him wanted to believe the fantasy he felt when he looked at Sophie—the illusory promise of a real partnership. But that was impossible.

Physical passion was all he trusted a woman to give him now. And his desire for Sophie had reached such combustible levels.

If only she weren't so vulnerable from her mother's death he'd have suggested a temporary liaison for their mutual pleasure. That was all he would ever offer another woman.

But he couldn't in all honour seduce a girl whose grief for her mother was so fresh and painful.

It had been hell resisting her. And never more so than just now, when she'd stepped close and he'd had to summon every atom of will-power so as not to sweep her close and do something she might regret later.

'You've got it wrong.' His voice emerged as rough as gravel.

'Have I? I've seen the photo of your wife in Eleni's room. I know how similar we are.'

'No!' He paused, shocked by her mistake, searching for the words to explain without revealing the past which he and his daughter had to live with.

'At first glance, yes, there's a similarity. But not after that single, initial moment.'

Her eyes were wary and he wanted to reach out and fold her close, kiss her till the pain went away and the spark of desire ignited in her eyes.

He wanted this woman as he'd never wanted before. With a savage, gnawing hunger that threatened his pretensions to being a civilised man.

Sto Diavolo! She needed protecting from *him*.

'Fotini will always have an important place as the mother of my daughter,' he said slowly, choosing his words. 'But ours was not a love match. We both wanted marriage and it was expected that love would grow with time.' As it might have done if Fotini had been a different woman.

'But believe me, Sophie,' he looked down into her drowning, golden-brown eyes, 'when I look at you it's only you that I see. I can assure you *absolutely* that I'm not seeking a replacement for Fotini. And I never will.'

CHAPTER EIGHT

SOPHIE PUFFED AS she strode up the path to the house. The walk had been long and tiring but it hadn't brought the peace she craved.

She kept replaying in her mind that scene at Phaestos. How close she'd come to making an utter fool of herself. She'd been so needy, reaching out to Costas like that. So sure he felt the spark between them too.

She stumbled as she recalled his words—his vehemence when he'd declared he never wanted a replacement for Fotini.

In other words, he didn't want another woman in his life. He didn't want *her*.

Sophie cringed at the memory, but still she couldn't let it go. Try as she might to stop it, her mind kept circling back to that confrontation, trying to make sense of what had happened between them.

He'd been adamant that Sophie didn't remind him of Fotini and in that, at least, she believed him. The dawning horror on his face at her words had been unmistakable.

He'd said the marriage wasn't a love match, but in the next breath had told her no one could replace his wife.

There was more to this, surely. Something he hadn't explained.

But what right did she have to pursue it any further? Her heart squeezed tight in her chest as she faced the fact that she had no rights at all where Costas Palamidis was concerned.

But Costas was a hard man to ignore and those persistent daydreams, of her held close in his arms, kept intruding no matter how hard she fought them.

He was a devoted father, spending much of the day with Eleni. As far as Sophie could tell he stayed on the estate, dealing with urgent business by phone and email. Which meant she had to work hard to avoid him.

With every cool glance and formal smile he sent her way he made it clear that he didn't want or need her sympathy or her company. That she was here for one thing only, the precious bone marrow which, if all went well, she'd be able to give his daughter.

Sophie blinked back the ready tears that were inevitably close these days. It was as if she'd somehow lost an outer protective layer that had muted her emotions during the traumatic weeks of her mother's illness.

Now, without its shield, she felt vulnerable, scraped raw by the strong currents of pain and need that tugged her this way and that.

Her time with Eleni was special, as was the tenuous, but real relationship that was building between them. Eleni was a little darling, full of pluck and with a cheeky sense of humour that Sophie envied.

As each day passed, she had to fight harder against her feelings for Costas. Back in Sydney it had been anger she'd felt for him, and a touch of fear too, if she was honest. Then had come a reluctant fellow feeling, when she realised what pain he hid behind his iron-hard exterior.

And through it all a potent awareness unlike anything she'd experienced before.

Now there was more. A growing tenderness as she watched him battle his inner demons and focus all his energies on his daughter. The sight of the pair of them together, one so big and tough and capable, and the other so fragile, yet so feisty, never failed to wring her heart.

Her every sense went on alert when he came near. The deep rasp of his voice sent a thrill through her. And, despite his rejection, she knew she'd do anything she could to smooth away the worry lines on his brow and the stiff, unyielding set of his shoulders that told her of the grief he carried. For his daughter. And for his wife.

Sophie sighed and took the path up to the house.

She didn't understand all that he felt for Fotini but of course he still grieved for her.

What a fool Sophie was. Wanting to help him through the pain that only time could heal.

As if she had some secret remedy for grief!

Her own sense of loss was a tangible thing, a deep, still well of pain that woke her early each morning. Yet here in the Palamidis home there was peace too, a sense of purpose that helped her day by day.

She shook her head. This situation was fraught with emotions and needs she barely understood. All she knew for sure was that she'd stay as long as she was needed.

Darkness was closing in as she entered the house but it would be a while yet before dinner. She didn't meet anyone as she crossed the ground floor and headed for the stairs. Evening settled like a blanket on the house, deepening its shadows, as she emerged into her corridor on the first floor.

Something made her pause, a muffled sound she couldn't identify. It came from the other wing, where Costas and Eleni had their rooms. Sophie hesitated a moment, then swung round. If Eleni had gone to bed perhaps she was having a bad dream.

There was no repeat of the noise, just silence as she slowed her steps and stopped outside Eleni's room.

Sure enough, there she was, tucked up with a teddy bear in a canopied bed with gossamer hangings that was every little girl's dream. A night-light glowed already in one corner and a tumble of toys on the huge window-seat was testament to a late play hour.

Sophie stood in the doorway, one hand on the jamb, as she watched Eleni's chest rise and fall. Her mouth wore a tiny smile and she'd hooked her plush bear up under one arm so it nestled beneath her chin.

Something caught in Sophie's throat as she stood there. A fierce, protective surge of emotion held her still.

That was why it took a few moments to realise she wasn't alone. The barest of movements caught her eye and she turned her head to see Costas hunched in a chair behind the door.

His elbows were on his splayed knees and his head was in his hands.

He made no sound. Didn't move. And in the soft light she could almost have sworn that he didn't even breathe, so still was he.

But not at peace.

There was despair in every line of his large frame. In the fingers tunnelled through his shining dark hair, in the slump of his broad shoulders. And in the droop of his neck.

He looked like a man defeated. A man who'd lost all hope. Not at all like the Costas Palamidis she knew.

And she couldn't bear it.

Softly she took a step towards him, and another. After a bare moment's hesitation she let her hand fall to his shoulder, moulding the hard ridge of wide muscle above the bone. Its rigidity confirmed what she'd seen. He was close to the end of his tether.

His head shot up at her touch, his dark gaze fixed on hers with an intensity that made her throat close, her breath catch. There was such fierce pain in his expression.

She let her hand slide along his broad shoulder to the stiff muscles of his neck, as if she could stroke some of the tension away. The heat of his flesh against hers seemed shockingly intimate.

She opened her mouth to speak but he put his finger to his lips.

She glanced across at Eleni, still sleeping soundly. In that moment he moved, clamping his hand over hers and dragging it to his side as he rose from the seat to tower above her. His hand, hard and unyielding, engulfed hers.

He pulled her out of the room, into the dusky corridor where the shadows lengthened. He didn't stop till they reached the curve in the hall that turned towards her room. Then he halted abruptly and stood, staring silently down at her.

His eyes glittered dark as night but she couldn't discern his expression.

'Are you all right?' she asked before she had time to think twice. 'Can I get you anything?' She took a tiny pace closer, tilting her chin up and trying to read his face, but it gave nothing away. Even his eyes were blank. She could have been looking into chips of pure obsidian for all the emotion she could find there.

What could she get him anyway? How would a cup of coffee or even a shot of alcohol help a man watching his daughter fight for her life?

She was foolish even to try reaching out to him. He'd made it abundantly clear that he didn't want her understanding. Or her presence.

It was time she left.

She tugged at his hand to release his hold. But his fingers didn't loosen their grip.

'Forget I—'

'Yes, there is something,' he murmured, his voice a low, dark thread of sound that sent a shard of tension through her.

Sophie stared up at him, saw the moment when his eyes lit with a flash of life. Like fire in a frozen wasteland. But the sight of that blaze brought no comfort.

Something very like fear trickled inch by inch down her spine as she watched his expression change, his lips curve up into a wolfish smile.

'What—'

'This,' he hissed as his head plunged down and his lips took hers.

Fire. Flaring need. A maelstrom of sensations assaulted her. His lips so soft yet so demanding. His searing breath, burning like an invader's bombardment.

And deep within her a quivering awareness that *this* was what she'd wanted from him. This frightening, glorious passion.

He cupped her face in his big hands, holding it still while he turned his head and slanted his mouth hard over hers. And then he was inside. His tongue boldly seductive, inviting her to respond to his flagrantly erotic invitation.

And of course she did.

Swirling heat roared through her, loosening her muscles and her inhibitions. A sweet, yearning ache began deep in her womb and her skin prickled all over. Her nipples tightened.

She pressed into his kiss, drunk on the taste of him, dark and strong and erotically addictive.

Sophie welcomed him with her lips, her tongue, as if he was no stranger, but the centre of all her yearning, all her secret dreams.

His kiss was bold, unrepentant. Yet there was an underlying tenderness, a sensitivity to her own responses, that lulled her into surrender.

If she'd been thinking straight she would have pushed away from him. Denied the tell-tale excitement she felt at his touch. But Sophie wasn't thinking. She was drowning in sensations, floating on a tide of glorious passion. Excited by the aura of his severe strength, tightly leashed.

His hands threaded through her hair and his lips trailed down to the corner of her jaw, to the erogenous zone beneath her ear, and she sighed.

Giving in to the inevitable, she let her hands slide up his chest, revelling in the way his breath hitched in his throat at their slow, delicious progress. Ribbed muscle, solid chest, up to the hot skin of his neck and his dark, silky hair. Her fingers splayed on the back of his skull and she sought his mouth again.

Heaven!

This time the thrust of his tongue was more insistent, blatantly demanding.

And still she couldn't get close enough to him. The edgy, unsettling sensation in the pit of her stomach intensified. She shifted her weight, trying to ease that indefinable ache, even as she returned his kiss with a passion equal to his own.

His thigh brushed hers. He stepped closer. Sophie felt his body lean in towards hers. His heat pressed against her from shoulder to hip.

And then, on a surge of energy, he crowded her back against the wall, trapping her with his weight so that she couldn't move, even if she'd sought escape. Her breasts were crushed against him. Her breathing shallowed, but she didn't want him to move away.

The feel of him, solid and hot along the length of her body, evoked a passion she'd never known before. She wriggled nearer. Immediately he pushed one heavy thigh forward, holding her still. And then he jammed closer, so close she could hardly breathe, nudging her legs aside so that he could anchor himself within the cradle of her hips.

Right where the fire he'd stoked flared brightest.

Every inch of her burned. Burned for him. It was as inevitable as the ceaseless motion of the waves down on the shore. Nothing had ever felt so perfect, as if her body had known him before and was impatient to welcome him home.

It should have scared her. But Sophie was lost. There were no warning bells clanging in her brain, only the certain knowledge that this was *right*. And that it still wasn't enough. The musky scent of him, of powerful, uncompromising masculinity, should have made her pause, so blatant was it now as he clamped her body against his. But it only incited her starved senses. And when his hand swept down her side so knowingly, pressing into the curve of her waist, the swell of her hips, and back to tease the side of her breast, she was only aware of the sinuous push of her body into his touch, of her longing for him.

She stretched up against him, eager to match the demands of his mouth as it plundered hers.

Then he gripped her torso in both hands and lifted her higher, pinning her against the wall with his lower body. She gasped at the intimacy of his touch, his erection unmistakable between her legs, against her belly. And the need grew in her there, the restless, empty yearning for physical fulfilment.

His kiss became more potent, devastating in its ruthless sensuality, as he took her mouth, possessed it utterly. His heart pounded against her breasts, its rhythm like a racing train. Matching hers.

And then his hands slid round and cupped her breasts. Sophie sighed into his mouth. Darts of electric energy tingled from her nipples at his every caress and spread burning devastation along her nerves. To her womb. To her legs. To the juncture of her thighs that softened like warm butter against the press of his strength.

When he broke the kiss to press his lips to her throat, she gasped for air in huge, frantic mouthfuls. She was out of control, far beyond any mastery of her own body. She shuddered convulsively as he nipped her ear lobe, sending delicious tremors of awareness through her.

'You like this, Sophie?' His voice was a rasping, air-starved murmur that weakened her even more. Through the cotton fabric of her shirt he tweaked her nipple, creating another jolt of blazing excitement.

'Yes,' she breathed, her hands busy with their restless exploration of his muscled shoulders, so wide and so tense.

He lifted his head then to stare at her. His eyes glittered with a savage excitement that should have frightened her. Except that it matched her own. The laboured sound of their breathing echoed in the still hall.

'Good,' he said, his chest still heaving. 'Because that's what you can give me, Sophie.' He slid his hand down to her waist, insinuating it between them to brush across the front of her jeans, lower and lower, till she shuddered at the explicit contact.

She stared up into a face ravaged by raw need. No evidence of softness, of gentleness there. Only stark lust.

She shivered, but this time it wasn't with carnal excitement. Finally, too late, she realised she was dealing with a man who didn't give a damn for anyone or anything right now except the need for release.

'Sex, Sophie,' he breathed. His dark-as-sin eyes locked with hers. 'That's what I want. That's *all* I want from you.'

She watched his lips move, heard the words, yet somehow she couldn't take them in.

But if she sought something else, some shred of tenderness, some deeper emotion from this man, she was doomed to disappointment. His eyes were febrile with lust. And nothing else. His face had a tightly drawn quality that proclaimed the extremity of his need. Pure physical desire. Nothing else.

What else had she expected?

Cold, hard, unwanted reality doused the roaring inferno that had held her spellbound.

She slumped, her hands still grasping his shoulders for support. He let her slide down the wall so she could stand on her own two feet.

Yet she would have collapsed in a heap if not for his possessive hold on her. Her knees shook as if she'd run a marathon.

'Nothing to say, Sophie?' His lips twisted in a humourless smile that finally eliminated the last trace of burgeoning excitement that had grown inside her during their kiss.

All her desperate desire was extinguished as suddenly and completely as a candle snuffed out in a strong wind. She felt hollow, as if something vital had been scooped out of her at his words, and at the emptiness she read in his features.

An emptiness that echoed inside her.

She'd been a fool. A blind, unthinking fool.

There was nothing here for her. She knew it now, without his words. Yet he said them anyway. And each syllable was like a nail hammering into her vulnerable, foolish heart.

'I don't want your sympathy,' he said. 'There's no place in my life for that.' He drew in a mighty breath and paused.

'But I'll take your body, Sophie. Every gorgeous centimetre of it. I want to lose myself in your softness. I want to forget the world for an hour. For a single night. But that's all. It's oblivion I want, Sophie. Sex and ecstasy and simple, animal pleasure. Nothing else. Not feelings or tenderness. No relationship. No future.'

He swiped his thumb over her nipple, once, twice, deliberately, while he stared down at her with a face darkened by pure need. She shuddered in unwilling response to his touch. Her body was so weak. She was appalled not by the ferocity of his stare, but by the shameful realisation that she still wanted him, still responded to him, even though he'd made it unequivocally clear that he didn't want *her*. That any warm, willing female body would satisfy him right now.

And she felt ashamed of what she'd done. Of how she'd responded to him so uninhibitedly.

'So, Sophie. Will you give me what I want? What I've craved ever since I saw you? Will you give me sweet oblivion?'

Sophie opened her mouth. Tried to find the words. Any words that would end this. But nothing came. She gaped at him, still feeling the echo of desire thrumming through her body, remembering the ecstasy of their mutual need.

But now she felt cheapened by it. He'd made her feel like a whore.

She'd reached out to him, wanting to help, to ease his pain and share his burden. And, she realised with brutal honesty that cut through all her instinctive excuses, she'd craved his affection, had wanted to build a relationship, however fragile, with this complex, difficult man who'd taken control of her life from the moment he stalked into it a mere week ago.

Yet all the while he'd seen her as nothing more than a convenient female body. Lips and breasts and hips to be enjoyed for a moment's pleasure then discarded.

He didn't want *her*. Didn't need *her*. Not her brain or her heart or the person she was, still trying to come to grips with her life.

She drew a shuddering breath, ignoring the bone-deep pain that lanced through her chest.

At least he was honest. She should be thankful he'd spelled it all out for her now, before she'd been swept away by his ardour and by her own longing. A longing for love, she now realised, turning her head away, unable to meet his piercing stare.

His hands tightened around her ribs, their span heavily possessive. 'Is that a no?' he drawled. But she heard the urgency behind his contempt.

And, lord help her, it wouldn't take much for her to give in and offer him what he wanted. Not when her body responded to his as if they were soul mates. She didn't doubt for an instant that physically it would be glorious.

And then how would she feel? It didn't bear thinking about.

Sophie slid her hands down from his shoulders and shoved with all her might. She had to get away. Now.

For a few fraught moments he didn't budge. She didn't have the strength to shift him, despite her growing desperation.

And then, abruptly, he stepped back, his eyes shadowed and unreadable. Her hands fell to her sides.

She didn't remember running down the hallway to the sanctuary of her room, of locking the door, or stripping off and standing under a shower so hot surely it must cleanse her.

All she knew was that she'd left her self-respect behind with Costas Palamidis.

CHAPTER NINE

COSTAS PACED THE sitting room, flicking another impatient glare at his watch. Where was she? The sun was already riding low in the west and still she hadn't returned.

Sophie had been out since early morning. Surely she should be back by now?

He paused in front of the picture window, scowling as he stared out at the silver-grey olive grove and the glitter of the sea.

She'd sneaked down for breakfast almost before the staff was awake. Slipped out of the house and told the housekeeper merely that she would be out for the day.

And she'd taken Yiorgos with her. He didn't know whether to be glad she wasn't alone or furious with jealousy.

It was no good. He had so little control where Sophie was concerned. She intruded on his thoughts all the time. She was there in his mind when he carried Eleni on his shoulders down through the orchard to the sea. And there as he'd tucked his daughter in for her nap, fielding her interminable, sulky questions about where Sophie was today and why she hadn't come to play.

He'd known the answer to that. And his flesh crawled as he thought of it now.

She was avoiding him. It was a wonder she hadn't disappeared completely, not just escaped for a day. Not after what he'd done to her.

He spun on his foot and strode the length of the massive

room, along the corridor and through the door that led outside. He stood on the stone steps in the warmth of the late sun, breathing hard as if he'd just sprinted a couple of kilometres. He scrubbed his hand over his face and up to tunnel through his hair.

But he couldn't hide from it. The guilt that had dogged him since last night. Since he'd kissed Sophie. Since he'd almost ravaged her with a hunger more befitting a beast than a civilised man.

He'd deliberately taken advantage of her worry and sympathy, allowing his needy, selfish desires to drive him. When he'd felt her hand on him, her gentle, soothing touch to his shoulder, and when he'd seen the answering pain in her soft eyes as he'd sat beside Eleni's bed, his control had finally snapped.

In one writhing, overpowering, unstoppable wave, his need had risen and consumed him. Consumed them both. All he'd known was that he had to get her away from his daughter's room. That they needed some vestige of privacy for what was between them.

But he hadn't even made it further than the open hallway!

Costas swallowed down the bitter taste of self-loathing and stepped away down the path, striding out as if he could somehow escape the knowledge of his own guilt. But of course that was impossible.

Hell! Even now he could see the distress in her eyes. The horrified recoil as he'd told her exactly what he wanted from her. At every deliberately brutal, cruel word she'd winced, her pupils dilating with pain. He'd taken her charity and thrust it back at her, making it a tainted thing. As tainted as his own lust for her.

No matter that his body had been rock hard with wanting her. And with the effort of control needed to prevent himself from taking her then and there, without preliminaries, in the corridor. No matter that his soul ached for the comfort he knew she alone could give him, for the touch of her soft hands against his flesh. He'd known that touch intimately every night in his turbulent dreams. And in his waking fantasies. He craved the reality of it as the parched earth craved soft, sweet rain at the end of the long summer drought.

No matter that she tasted like an angel. So miraculously sweet that he was addicted after just one kiss. Or that she responded to him so completely, so ferociously that his soul cried out in wonder and delight.

His woman. Those were the crazy, impossible words that had pounded through his numbed, awed brain as he drank in the taste of her, imprinted her soft curves against his rampant body. That was the knowledge that had throbbed through his pulse and made his hands quiver.

His.

Even now the primitive, potent need to possess her lay barely suppressed. He wanted to reach out and take her. Hold her fast. Claim her for his own. It was a certainty that defied logic, but resided bone-deep in his body, soul-deep in his psyche.

He emerged from a thicket onto the bare top of the small headland, came to a stop on the edge of the cliff that dropped down to the shallow curve of the bay. The tang of salt was on his lips. The sound of waves rolling in was heavy and more regular than his own heartbeat.

He strove for cool logic. The fire in his blood, the proprietorial instinct…they'd clouded his brain. It was simply a volatile surge of lust he experienced.

She was no more his woman than he was the man of her dreams.

He owed all his allegiance to his daughter. He had no time for anyone else in his life. Much less a girl with her own life far away in Australia. A girl grieving for her mother, wounded by the memories of family conflict and rejection.

A girl so passionate and independent that he felt more alive just talking with her, arguing and debating and finally finding common ground, than he had in a long time.

He shook his head. He was deluding himself. They were strangers brought together by circumstance. That was all.

That was why he'd been so brutally frank with her last night. Describing his aching need in blatant physical terms, each word designed to shred their growing intimacy and make her shun him. For he knew one thing: he'd lost his own battle to retain his honour.

That was why he'd deliberately provoked her disgust of him.

It was the only barrier left between them. But even as he'd done it, giving her every excuse to hate him, he'd teetered on a knife edge, almost wishing she wouldn't care. That she'd lead him to her room anyway and take him to paradise.

No decent man would seduce a guest in his house, a young woman already battling her own pain with a grace and inner strength that must draw respect. No honourable man would take advantage of her empathy to force himself on her.

Yet he would have taken her last night, grateful for the solace of her body, the sweet sensuality of her response. Even hating his weakness, he would have had her. Not once but right through the long, aching hours of darkness.

His body hardened at the memory of her against him. He should be grateful that she'd shown the will-power he lacked and removed herself from his vicinity.

Yet he couldn't stifle his restless unease. Her absence was even worse than the torment of having her close at hand.

'Not far now,' Yiorgos said with a quick smile.

The words were like a douche of chill water to Sophie's spirits. Soon they'd be back at the Palamidis villa and she'd have to face Costas.

She chewed on her lip, wondering how she was going to brazen it out. How could she see him again after what had happened last night? Now he knew just how weak she was. She'd almost crawled up his body, so impetuous in her need to get close to him. He'd kissed her, held her in his arms, and she'd lost all control. Had offered herself to him, there in the hallway, without thought.

It had only been his words, pounding into her desire-numbed brain, that finally brought her to her senses.

And even then, even when he looked at her with the easy contempt of a man who knew she was his for the taking, it had been an almost insurmountable struggle to tear herself away. Despite his words, despite the pain they inflicted, she'd still wanted him.

What sort of woman did that make her?

'*Thespinis?* Are you all right?'

She turned to Yiorgos, noting the genuine concern in his flashing eyes. He'd been a pleasant companion all day, even though she hadn't been able to convince him to call her by her name. The boss wouldn't like it, he said. And that settled the matter, of course. The boss obviously got whatever he wanted.

Except her.

'I'm OK,' she said, dredging up a smile. 'Maybe just a little tired.'

He grinned then, flicking her a mischievous glance. 'I don't see how that could be. After all it was only the markets you visited. And then the archaeological museum. And Knossos. And—'

'You've made your point,' Sophie said, and this time her smile was real. 'It's been a wonderful day. Thank you.'

'It was my pleasure. Any time. You just ask and I'll drive you wherever you want to go.'

Sophie watched as he concentrated on a tight curve in the road. He really was remarkably good-looking. Gorgeous even, with those large, laughing eyes. And he was close enough to her own age for her to relax in his company and enjoy his jokes.

So why didn't she feel even a spark of attraction to him?

Why did his handsome face leave her unmoved, when just the memory of Costas' hard, passionate features and dark, probing eyes made her feel as if something had unravelled in the pit of her stomach?

And why did eagerness mix with her trepidation at the prospect of seeing him again?

Fortunately Yiorgos chose that moment to regale her with another of his stories, distracting her from thoughts she'd rather avoid. And soon she was laughing so much that she didn't even notice that they'd swung through the security gates to the estate.

It was only as they rounded a gentle curve in the long private road and the house came into view that she realised they were back.

And that Costas was waiting for them.

He stood, arms akimbo, at the head of the steps. A forbidding figure that dominated the scene.

Sophie's grin morphed into a rictus stretch of taut lips, all laughter fled. Would she ever see the man and not experience that desperate, melting awareness deep inside?

He was down the steps and opening the passenger door even as the limousine drew to a gentle halt.

'Where have you been?' His hand fastened on her elbow, drawing her from her seat as soon as she'd released her seat belt.

'Sightseeing,' she said, raising her eyes to his. They were unreadable. Pure, impenetrable black. But the scowl on his face needed no interpretation. He was furious. His brows tilted down at a ferocious angle and the grip on her elbow was more than supportive. It was like a vice, clamped hard round her arm.

She shrugged, but he didn't break his hold. Instead he bent low to the open car door and snapped a barrage of staccato Greek at his chauffeur. It was too rapid for her to understand, but she could tell by the suddenly sombre look on Yiorgos' face that it was far from pleasant.

What was Costas' problem?

'I'm sorry,' she interrupted, 'I didn't know you needed the car today.'

Costas straightened to stare down at her. A flash of dark emotion in his eyes made her shiver. The controlled energy he projected made her hackles rise. She sensed he was waiting for the right moment to pounce.

'I didn't,' he cut in succinctly. 'And I have more than one car, should I need one. But I would have appreciated knowing where you were. I expected you back hours ago.'

What? He'd been worried about her? Surely not. Not when he glared at her so disapprovingly.

'I didn't know I had to report my movements to you.'

She was damned if she'd apologise again. He'd offered the use of the car and now he was annoyed she'd used it. Was he worried his precious bone-marrow donor might disappear off the island if he didn't keep tabs on her?

'Why did you switch the cellphone off? What were you up to all that time?' He thrust his head close to hers. She could see the

The Reader Service™ — Here's how it works:

Accepting the free books places you under no obligation to buy anything. You may keep the books and gift and return the despatch note marked 'cancel'. If we do not hear from you, about a month later we'll send you 6 brand new books and invoice you just £2.80* each. That's the complete price - there is no extra charge for postage and packing. You may cancel at any time, otherwise every month we'll send you 6 more books, which you may either purchase or return to us - the choice is yours.

*Terms and prices subject to change without notice.

tic of a rapid pulse at the base of his clenched jaw; smell the natural, masculine scent of him in her nostrils.

And feel the traitorous weakness of her reaction to him. The recognition of it was like a betrayal. How could she?

'We went into the mountains this afternoon, *Kyrie Palamidis*,' Yiorgos said from inside the car. 'We lost the signal.'

'And you could always have left a message,' she interrupted, 'if it was anything important.'

Costas flicked her a momentary glance then said something curtly dismissive to Yiorgos and slammed the car door shut. He still held her arm in a tight grip as the engine purred into life and the car headed round the corner of the house towards the garages.

'Did you know that Yiorgos is engaged to be married?' he said in a lethally quiet voice.

She frowned. What had that to do with anything?

'Did you know?' His fingers bit into her flesh and she winced. Immediately he loosened his grip. But he didn't release her.

'No, I didn't.' She glared up at him, wondering what the hell was going on.

He nodded once. 'Then perhaps I should tell you that his fiancée is a very possessive, very jealous young woman.'

For a couple of seconds Sophie stared at him, her jaw sagging as the implications of his words permeated her brain. He was warning her off? What did he think she was, some sort of seductress who'd gone straight from the boss to the chauffeur?

Nausea churned her stomach, welled in her throat. His tone was as icy as his eyes were hot, and she felt as if he'd just slapped her, hard.

In that instant she realised just what sort of woman Costas thought her.

'Get your hands off me!' she hissed.

Surprisingly, this time he complied, leaving her free to escape up the stairs, almost stumbling in her haste to seek sanctuary.

Well done, Palamidis. Costas watched her scramble inside as if the hound of Hades himself were after her.

Sto Diavolo! He couldn't have done worse if he'd tried!

He planted his feet wide, refusing to give in to the instinct that told him to race after her and gather her close. The last thing she needed was him invading her space. Not when he'd hurt her again, insulted her out of sheer, bloody, dog-in-the-manger jealousy.

It had taken just one glance at her smiling face, the carefree laughter in her eyes as she responded to Yiorgos, and the look on his driver's face as he watched her, and Costas had lost it.

Jealous of his driver!

She was so beautiful when she smiled like that, all vestige of strain disappearing from her face, that it had struck him like a blow, deep and devastating in his chest. It hurt, knowing she'd never look at him in that way, smile so freely and approvingly. He'd sacrificed that last night when he'd behaved like a thug.

But no man could fail to recognise the male appreciation in Yiorgos' eyes as he turned on the charm for her. More than appreciation. There'd been speculation. And it was that look that had drawn Costas' simmering anger to the surface, making him lash out indiscriminately.

He shook his head. He should have saved his anger for Yiorgos. Hell, the guy was a practised womaniser with a reputation envied by half the local men.

Costas would have a few choice words with him soon.

And in future he, Costas, would drive Sophie wherever she wanted to go.

He straightened his shoulders and started up the steps. In the meantime he had an apology to make.

Eventually he located her, emerging from a downstairs powder room. Her shoulders were hunched and her eyes skittered from his. Her mouth was a taut line of pain in her overly pale face.

He'd done that. Damn his possessive masculine ego!

'Sophie…' He reached for her hand but she jerked away, retreating a step till she'd backed up to a wall.

Sick to the stomach, he let his hand drop to his side.

'What do you want?' Her tone was weary. She stared at a point somewhere near his chin.

'I need to apologise.' The words were rough, dragged from him by the sight of her hurt.

Fleetingly her eyes met his and her lips curved in a surprised circle that tightened the curl of need deep in the pit of his stomach. He drew a long breath.

'I was annoyed with my driver, not you,' he said. 'He should have known to keep in contact. In future you have only to ask and I'll take you wherever you wish to go.'

Silence.

'I'm sorry you thought I was implying—'

'What? That I was a tramp?'

She met his eyes now and the turbulent mix of emotions he saw there, the anguish and the shocked fury, seared his conscience.

She hurried on before he could formulate a response. 'That because I'd decided not to go to bed with you last night, I must be eager for a little fun and games with someone else?' Her voice was a searing, agonised whisper. 'What do you think I am? A bitch on heat?'

'Sophie, I—'

'Keep away from me.' She slapped away the hand he hadn't even noticed he'd held out to her.

There were tears in her eyes and her lower lip trembled. Pain twisted deep inside him as he watched her obvious distress. He'd done that to her, damn his black soul. He wanted nothing more than to kiss her hurt away.

'I said, stay away,' she hissed, as he closed the distance between them, reaching out to bracket her with his hands, flat on the wall beside her head. The tantalising shimmer of liquid gold in her eyes ensnared him. Her delicate, fresh scent encompassed him, and the warmth of her luscious body drew him like a magnet.

He hefted one massive breath and struggled against the compulsion to reach out and claim her. To brand her as his own.

'That's the problem, Sophie. I can't keep my distance. Not

any more.' He dragged in another juddering breath. 'Don't you understand?'

He stared down into her wide stunned eyes and knew he was lost.

'Why do you think I was so furious with Yiorgos?'

'Because you thought I was seducing him,' she said flatly.

He shook his head.

She shifted her weight and shot a glance over his shoulder. 'I need to go and—'

'Why, Sophie?' he demanded.

Slowly, as if she fought with every ounce of her strength, she lifted her eyes to his. She looked impossibly weary. 'Because you don't want me out of your sight,' she whispered slowly then looked away.

He nodded, acknowledging the surge of ravening hunger that even now tore at the frayed remnants of his self-control. A good thing his hands were planted firmly against the plaster. It helped him resist the desire to use them to shape her face, her fragile neck, her delicate curves.

'And why is that?' he whispered, focusing on her convulsive swallow, on the way she tugged at her lower lip with her teeth.

'Because I'm the only person who might be able to help Eleni,' she murmured at last, still refusing to meet his gaze.

'Wrong.'

Her gaze shot up again at the single word. The instant connection between them was like a jolt of electricity, charging the air with pulsing anticipation.

'It's because I'm jealous,' he admitted, stripping his soul bare. His voice was a low animal growl that matched perfectly the savage possessiveness welling inside him. 'I'm jealous of anyone who has you to themselves when I don't.'

Her eyes widened and her mouth gaped and he wanted, more than anything, the ultimate luxury of taking her lush, enticing lips with his. His whole body trembled with barely repressed desire. Sweat hazed his skin at the effort it took to keep still, keep from sweeping her into his embrace and burying his face in her sweetly scented hair.

'Do you understand, Sophie?' His voice was raw, all pretence at civilised gloss scoured away by this elemental hunger. 'I was jealous of my driver because he spent the day alone with you. I didn't think for a minute you might be seducing him.'

He paused, gathering his courage.

'I wanted you to be seducing me.'

The stark admission reverberated in the still air between them. Blatant. Inescapable. Overpowering.

He'd never felt so driven, so desperate for a woman's touch. And even more, for her understanding.

He saw the warm colour flood her face, accentuate the high contours of her cheekbones. And he felt an answering heat, pooling low in his groin. Her eyes were wide, so clear and enticing that he felt he could lose himself in their promise, just as he wanted to lose himself in the heady temptation of her body.

He inhaled the scent of her, like beckoning spring after a long, cold winter. Enticing, promising, seductive.

He heard her soft breaths, short and rapid. And he could taste her already on his tongue. After last night he'd craved that taste with a frenzied longing that appalled him.

He had only to lift a hand, cup her face as he closed the distance between them and—

'*Kyrie Palamidis.*' The quiet voice of his housekeeper shattered the stillness.

The world tilted and shifted into focus again.

Till that moment it had been as if nothing else existed. There was only this space where he and Sophie stood, bound by a passion so strong it eclipsed all his puny self-control.

He blinked, drew himself up and turned.

The housekeeper stood at the end of the hall, near the door to the servants' quarters. She held a cordless phone in her hands and her eyes were wide with astonishment. Hastily she looked away.

In all the years she'd worked for him she'd never seen him with any woman other than Fotini. Even before his marriage, he hadn't been in the habit of seducing guests in his home.

'It's the hospital on the phone,' she explained.

Costas' heart leapt right up into his throat at her words.

The moment of reckoning had arrived. Something—fear—clutched at his chest, squeezing so tight that for a moment he couldn't breathe.

He felt Sophie's eyes on him and pushed back his shoulders, forced himself to move, to accept whatever news awaited.

He'd done what he could. Now he had to summon the strength to endure what he must.

He paced over and took the phone with a brief word of thanks. Then he turned and met Sophie's stare across the room.

'Costas Palamidis speaking,' he said, automatically switching to Greek.

'We have the result, sir.' He recognised the voice of Eleni's doctor. 'We'd like you to bring your daughter in for treatment as soon as possible. We believe the donor you found is compatible. We'll proceed with the transplant.'

CHAPTER TEN

COSTAS STARED THROUGH THE glass wall panel and felt a lump the size of a football lodge in his chest. He swallowed hard and forced down the welling emotion.

He'd coped with the trauma of the transplant procedure and the hard days that followed, helpless to do more than stay with Eleni through her discomfort. Through her raw, aching tiredness and the inevitable tears and upsets.

He'd done what he had to. Kept his emotions in check. He'd cajoled, encouraged, consoled.

And he'd been astounded at his little girl's strength and determination. She was so tiny. So incredibly fragile. Yet she had the heart of a lion. Possessed a fearlessness that far outstripped his own strength.

Through the long weeks since the transplant he'd held it all together: delegating control of his business empire, fending off Press intrusions, fielding endless queries from friends and relatives, doing what had to be done.

So why suddenly now did the sight of his daughter strike him so hard that it felt as if someone had grabbed his heart and tried to rip it out?

He braced himself against the wall, dragging in a tortured breath that sawed painfully into his lungs.

His palm was slippery with sweat. His arm trembled as he fought to brace himself. The cold, bitter taste of fear filled his mouth.

Even now no one knew if the transplant would save Eleni.

He raised his head and looked again into his daughter's hospital room. She was propped up against a bank of pillows, her tiny frame pathetically thin. Yet a smile lurked at the corners of her mouth and her eyes danced. She looked down at the huge picture book spread before her and said something he couldn't hear.

It must have been a joke. Even through the glass he heard the woman beside her give an answering laugh.

Sophie.

He couldn't see her smile—it was hidden by the surgical mask she wore. But he saw the way her eyes crinkled in delight at Eleni's comment. The way she tipped back her head, laughing with her whole body.

The ache inside him deepened, twisted. His pulse ratcheted up a notch, as it always did when she was near.

Sophie and Eleni. Eleni and Sophie.

He shook his head, as if he could clear the whirling tumble of emotions and half-formed thoughts bombarding him.

He'd seen them together before. Sophie visited every day. Eleni wanted her there, so she was one of the few people allowed into the quarantined room.

The pair of them had grown ever closer. That was obvious even though Sophie tried to time her visits to avoid him: for the rare occasions when he was snatching a nap or meeting with doctors.

Not that he could blame her. They hadn't been alone together since the afternoon he'd confronted her with his jealous rage.

After that it was a wonder she hadn't left. Technically there was nothing to keep her in Greece. Yet she hadn't taken him up on his offer of a flight to Sydney. Instead she'd stayed on.

For Eleni.

She certainly hadn't remained in Crete to be near him. Costas knew he'd been a brute. An unreasoning, foul-tempered lout. Yet he knew that, faced again with the same circumstances, he'd probably behave exactly the same.

'Costa?'

He swung round to see his mother hurrying towards him down the corridor.

'Has something happened? You look so—'

'Nothing's happened,' he reassured her. He straightened and turned his back on the wall of glass. 'There's no change. She seems to be doing reasonably well.'

'Then what's wrong?' She allowed herself to be drawn into his embrace and kissed him soundly on both cheeks.

'Nothing's wrong,' he lied.

His mother glanced into Eleni's room and smiled. 'It's good to see them together—they have a real bond. At first glance that girl is so like Fotini it's astounding. But the differences are strong beneath the surface.'

'We won't go there,' he murmured, but even to his own ears it sounded like a growl. He turned to the glass panel, seeing Sophie close the book and look up to find him watching her. Her whole body stilled.

He wished he could read her expression. Not just the blaze of molten gold in her widening eyes. They held his for a heartbeat, for two, so long that he almost forgot about his mother, standing there beside him.

'Hiding from the truth won't make it go away.'

He watched Sophie put the book down beside the bed, then turn to talk to Eleni.

'Believe me. I'm not hiding from anything.'

'Aren't you? Yet you scowl whenever you look at Sophie. And you still freeze out any conversation about Fotini.'

He swung round to stare at his mother. 'This is neither the time nor the place.'

'Then when *is* the time? You've avoided talking about Fotini ever since the accident.'

'There's nothing to discuss. But don't worry, I'm aware of the differences between Sophie and her cousin.' His body responded vigorously and constantly to those unique differences. 'Sophie is no spoiled heiress and she wasn't brought up to be shallow or selfish.'

'Costa! That's not what I meant. And it's not like you to be so harsh. Not after the way you supported Fotini. You did everything a husband could to help her. More than many men would have done.'

And what had that achieved? Despite his vigilance, his eternal patience, he hadn't saved her from herself.

Costas felt the familiar helpless anger in the hollow of his gut. Perhaps if he'd truly loved her—

'She had severe post-natal depression,' his mother said. He felt her hand on his sleeve and looked down at her neat fingers against the dark fabric. 'It was no one's fault that her condition escalated so uncontrollably.'

'I disagree,' he countered. 'My wife chose to disregard her medical advice and shun her family. If she hadn't tried to drink and party her way out of her illness she wouldn't have lost control and smashed her car.'

If only he'd been with her that night. He should have ignored Eleni's slight fever and left her to her nanny's care. He could have postponed the late teleconference to Singapore. He should have—

'It was *no one's* fault, son. You weren't responsible.' He heard the words as if from a distance.

'And Eleni's illness is no one's fault either.'

Yet he felt the flare of guilt deep inside. The fear that he'd failed his daughter.

The silence was punctuated only by the harsh sound of his breathing as he fought a vice-like grip around his chest. It was as if iron bands constricted his lungs, cutting off his oxygen.

'Don't blame yourself, Costa. You need time to heal. To learn to trust again.'

Sharply he lifted his head. So, they were back to Sophie.

He wondered what his mother would say if she knew precisely how much his body wanted to *trust* Sophie Paterson. How completely she'd got under his skin, dominating even his troubled sleep. How impossibly strong was the connection he felt with her.

But he'd learned his lesson well. Trust and partnership were illusions he could do without. He knew not to fall for their spurious promise.

No matter how much he was tempted to believe.

After his marriage the last thing he needed was a new relationship. Especially with another girl from the house of Liakos.

His mother shook her head then turned away and began the ritual of hand-washing and donning mask and gown ready to visit Eleni.

Costas stood rock-still, trying to salvage the tattered shreds of his control.

His mother had dredged up memories he'd tried so hard to bury. And tenuous, seductive hopes that had no place in his life. He was off-balance, teetering on the brink of a black abyss of turbulent emotions.

What was happening to him?

He was always in control. That was how he operated. This sudden uncertainty—the wretched, unfamiliar feelings—he hated it.

Almost as much as he hated this waiting game, waiting to see if Eleni would live or die.

He shrugged back his shoulders and lifted his head, disgusted with himself. This was no time for weakness.

He watched his mother enter the private room. He wouldn't follow her just yet. Eleni might pick up on his tension. Instead he'd go and check if the doctor was in. So far the medical staff had been cautiously optimistic, but noncommittal about Eleni's long-term recovery. It drove him crazy. He needed something more concrete.

He was moving down the corridor when he heard the door open behind him. He heard a murmur of voices then footsteps. It was Sophie.

He stopped, unable to help himself.

Sophie avoided his intense stare as she removed her mask and gown. It only took a few seconds. She wished it took longer—anything to delay their inevitable conversation.

She was a coward, she knew.

Especially when Costas Palamidis stood there, as imposing and as unapproachable as a stone idol.

She wondered what he was thinking. She hadn't missed the speculation in his eyes when he'd found her sitting with Eleni.

She should be furious with him for the way he'd treated her. She *was* furious.

But that insidious longing was stronger than ever. Shamefully so.

Even now, after so much time to pull herself together, to perfect a semblance of nonchalance when he was near, she felt the skitter of awareness, that thrill of self-destructive excitement under her skin.

And it was far worse now. For this time they were alone. No Eleni, no medical staff, no hovering relatives to fill the room and break the tension between them.

The tension was there all right. A taut awareness that vibrated like a wire humming between them. It made her movements choppy, uncoordinated. Her breath came in short, jagged gasps till she found the strength to regulate it.

Now wasn't the time to try to fathom Costas or the extraordinary hold he exerted over her. There'd never be a right time for that. She wasn't a masochist.

She needed to concentrate on something else. Like the duty she had to discharge. Just thinking about it made her nervous.

'Hello, Sophie.' His voice was as deep as ever, like the soft, low rumble of thunder in the distance.

'Costas.' She inclined her head, trying to seem unfazed by his liquid dark eyes and the way he loomed over her. 'Eleni seems a little brighter this afternoon,' she offered. 'She was laughing and there's colour in her cheeks.'

He nodded but his brooding gaze didn't leave her face.

'I'm about to go and check whether the results of the latest tests are back,' he said and she read fierce control in the grim lines bracketing his mouth.

She wished she could offer to go with him. To support him when he got whatever news was awaiting him.

How stupid was that? He didn't want her help, her sympathy. He'd made it abundantly clear that he didn't need anything from her except the use of her body for a night.

And yet, idiotically, she couldn't stop the surge of empathy for him as he stood alone, facing the dark, uncertain future.

She'd lain awake night after night wondering if that was the real reason she'd stayed in Crete. Not just because of little Eleni. But because Costas Palamidis needed someone.

Needed her.

She shook her head. How mind-blowingly pathetic could she get? The man had turned independence into an art form. And as for truly needing anyone as ordinary as her…

'Sophie? We need to talk. I—'

'I was wondering if you'd help me,' she burst out before he could continue. Anything to stop him. Whatever he was going to say, whatever trite apology or explanation he was going to make, she didn't want to hear it.

'I need to find another one of the private wards,' she said quickly. 'And I need to convince the nursing staff to let me in.'

'Your grandfather.' It wasn't a question.

'Yes.'

Her grandfather. The man she'd vowed never to forgive.

'You've decided to see him, then.' Costas' dark eyes bored into her, penetrating her defences, her would-be careless posture.

She shrugged. 'It seemed appropriate.'

The information Costas had given her about the old man and the discovery that he was here in this very hospital had irrevocably altered her daily visits. Knowing that she passed so close to the tyrant who'd shaped her mother's life. Gradually, almost imperceptibly, the guilt had come. It had been compounded by the vague feeling, after watching a valiant child struggle through each new day, that perhaps life was more important than old grudges.

An uncomfortable suspicion had grown inside her. However right she was in her judgement of Petros Liakos, life was too precious for feuds. Was she was growing into someone just as stubbornly cruel as he'd been to her mum?

She didn't intend to forgive him for what he'd done. But she couldn't be as pitiless as he'd been.

Maybe he wouldn't want a visit from her. That wouldn't be a surprise. But if he did, then she'd swallow her resentment and see him.

'Sophie?'

She looked up, wondering if she'd missed something Costas had said.

'Are you ready?' he murmured. 'I can show you the way, I've visited him myself.'

Of course. She'd forgotten Petros Liakos had been his wife's grandfather too. Costas would take such family obligations seriously, even after Fotini's death.

'Yes. Thanks.' She wasn't about to admit that she didn't think she'd ever be ready to face old man Liakos. That the thought of meeting him made her want to turn tail and run. Instead she fell into step beside Costas.

There was something strangely soothing about his easy, deliberate pace. His tall presence beside her generated a welcome heat that counteracted her sudden chill.

She was glad of his company. After avoiding him for so long, trying not even to think about him, she felt better just having him beside her as she went to face the man she'd hated and resented most of her life.

Surreptitiously she watched Costas. So aloof, so impenetrable. He stared ahead down the corridor and she saw strength etched in his profile, in the way he held himself.

She knew without doubt that his was a different strength to her grandfather's. He had no need to prove himself by manipulating people weaker than himself. By playing vicious games with their lives.

Costas was a man who allowed himself to be tender with those he loved—his daughter and his mother. She'd seen it in his amazing gentleness when he was with them.

For one soul-searing, painful moment she let herself wish he'd extend that loving protectiveness to encompass her.

But that would never happen.

She and Costas were doomed to rub each other up the wrong way—to strike sparks. From the first he'd awakened reactions so intense that she'd known at some primitive level he was dangerous. She'd been fighting him one way or another ever since.

So how could she be drawing strength now from his presence?

Sophie gave up trying to fathom that conundrum. Nothing about their relationship was logical or moderate. It was all high emotion and raw passion—running hot in her blood. It had nothing to do with her mind.

Even now, as he led the way to another floor, passing ward staff and visitors, the two of them were essentially alone, cocooned in a private world where everything else faded into a background blur. He didn't touch her. Yet she was aware with every alert nerve of his lithe form beside her, the swing of his arm so close to her own, the way he tempered his pace to match hers.

They rounded a corner and stopped in front of a nursing station. Sophie clawed for mental control as she realised they were here, at Petros Liakos' ward.

She couldn't face the old man with her mind fixed on Costas. She needed her wits about her, and every ounce of self-assurance she'd learned at her mother's knee.

Sophie straightened her shoulders, only half listening to the conversation between Costas and the nurse. She knew that facing this one, sick old man would test her resolve to the limits. But she owed it to her mother to be calm. To show him that her mother's daughter was a woman to be reckoned with, not brushed aside as unworthy.

She shouldn't care what he thought, but deep down she knew she did.

Her heart raced at a staccato beat. Dampness bloomed at her palms and she swiped them down the back of her jeans.

'Sophie?' Costas stared down at her. 'It's supposed to be one visitor at a time, but I'll come in with you.'

'No!' She shook her head. 'No, that's OK. I'd rather see him alone.'

She couldn't even begin to imagine facing both Petros Liakos and Costas together. She'd be a nervous wreck! And more than that, this confrontation was far too private, too personal, to be shared.

'It will be easier with me there,' he persisted. 'The stroke— it's affected his speech.'

She nodded. 'You forget I'm a trained speech pathologist. I'm used to working with speech impediments. And,' she hurried on before he could interrupt, 'as long as he speaks slowly I'll understand simple Greek.'

'You won't need to. Your grandfather speaks English.'

Now, that surprised her. She'd imagined him such an old-fashioned patriarch that he wouldn't concede the value of learning any language other than his own.

'*Kyrie Liakos* will see you now,' said the nurse, emerging from a room near by. Her eyes were fixed on Costas. She didn't even glance in Sophie's direction.

'Thank you,' Sophie said, walking towards the room.

'Sophie—' Costas sounded as if he'd like to say more.

'I'll see you later,' she said before he could continue and slipped into the private ward, letting the door close behind her.

It felt different from Eleni's bright hospital room.

Immediately the familiar too-sweet scent of sick-room flowers filled her nostrils, making her stomach churn. The intense, distinctive quiet that accompanied the gravely ill enveloped her.

For a long, awful interval the memories of her mother's deathbed rose to swamp her. Bitter nausea made her reel, her hand outstretched to the door behind her for support. Her skin prickled hotly and she swallowed down bile.

Then she blinked and the *déjà vu* eased. The resemblance between this suite and her mother's spartan room were few. Every inch here attested to a luxury unlike anything the Paterson family had been able to command.

But despite that it was a hospital room. The nearby oxygen tank, the drip, the panel of emergency buttons and dials beside the bed—they were all familiar.

Despite Petros Liakos' wealth, he was as powerless against illness as her mother had been.

There was complete silence as she concentrated on getting her breathing under control.

A curtain hid the head of the bed. Was he even awake? There was no movement, no rustle of sheets.

But the nurse had said he'd see her. He must be lying there now, waiting for her. Perhaps guessing she was too nervous to face him.

Sophie tilted up her chin and clenched her fists at her sides. If Petros Liakos could bear to look her in the eye, she wouldn't deny him the opportunity.

Slowly she paced towards the bed. Ridiculous to feel so nervous. She had nothing to be ashamed of!

The bedcovers shaped feet, long legs, a thin body. A big, gnarled hand lay on the coverlet, curled into a claw.

Tingling heat seared her skin as she paused, imagining how the owner of a hand like that, once strong and capable, could bear his body's incapacity. It must be hell.

She walked closer, to the end of the bed, and then she saw him. Petros Liakos, her mother's father. Patriarch of the Liakos family.

The man who'd disowned his flesh and blood because he'd refused to relinquish control over his daughter's life.

Glittering dark eyes met hers and she felt the force of his will-power, the surge of energy, even from where she stood. His heavy brows jutted low in a ferocious scowl. His nose was a prominent, commanding beak, just what you'd expect of a power-hungry tyrant.

Thank heaven she hadn't inherited that nose, Sophie thought hysterically, her mind shutting down against the turmoil of desperate emotion deep within.

Movement caught her eye. A clumsy, abrupt gesture from that useless fist on the bedclothes. She heard the hiss of his indrawn breath, recognised the savage sound of pure frustration. A man as proud as him would hate being seen like this.

Sophie looked up to his face again. This time she saw the rest, not the power she'd looked for and found the first time, but the frailty. The old man's cheeks were sunken, the skull too prominent beneath his skin. His mouth was distorted into a lopsided grimace.

A twist of sympathy knotted her stomach.

'Come to…gloat.' His voice was laboured, barely intelligible with its slurred consonants. She had to lean forward to hear it.

'No.' She stared straight back into his eyes. They seemed the only thing about him still alive.

He drew a deep, shuddering breath that racked his frail body and scoured her conscience. Maybe she should leave. He was in pain.

'Come…for my…money,' he mumbled.

'No!' She stood straighter, anger driving out unwilling sympathy.

She glared at him, feeling the hurried beat of her pulse as long moments passed.

'I was curious,' she said at last when she could control her voice.

Again that stifled gesture with his useless claw of a hand.

'Closer,' he whispered. 'Come closer.'

Sophie stepped up to the head of the bed, looking down at her grandfather propped against the mountain of pillows. This close his eyes looked febrile, glittering. It took her a moment to realise it was moisture that made his eyes so bright. Tears.

She stared, dumbfounded at the thought of this man crying. He must have seen the shock on her face, for he blinked and turned his head away, towards the window.

Sophie stared at his grizzled, still curly hair, and wondered if that had been genuine emotion she'd seen or simply the effect of his stroke.

'Look like…her.' He struggled to get the words out, as if the impediment of an almost useless tongue had got worse.

Silence throbbed between them, beating down against her like a weapon.

She felt numb. No, not numb. She felt *everything*. Fear, resentment, despair, grief. And something else, a grudging link she couldn't explain.

'Look…like…Christina.'

Her breath snared in her throat at his words.

He turned his head to glower at her, his eyes fiercer than ever.

But now she suspected that look was a mask designed to hide whatever emotions he felt as he stared back at her.

'Sit.' It was an order, despite his weak voice.

Sophie held his gaze, knowing that they were both remembering her mother.

She reached out a hand and drew forward the visitor's chair. Then she sat down beside her grandfather.

CHAPTER ELEVEN

THE SUN HAD dropped out of sight, leaving only the pellucid afterglow of twilight to show the cliff path.

Sophie breathed in the salty air, drawing the aromatic scent of wild herbs and the sea down deep into her lungs. So different from the antiseptic smell of the hospital.

She wrapped her arms tight round herself, hugging back the pain, dismayed at the welter of confused emotions that bombarded her. Each day they grew stronger.

Today had been no different from any other. An early walk along the shore and then her hospital visit. A few minutes' polite, stilted conversation with Costas as she left Eleni's room. Nothing extraordinary. And yet...today she felt raw, rubbed bare by intense emotion.

She should feel optimistic. Eleni looked brighter by the day, was making steady progress. Even her grandfather had gathered strength since her first visit. And a relationship of sorts was developing gradually, almost grudgingly, between them.

Sophie turned her face towards the sea breeze and shut her eyes, seeking peace from her confused thoughts.

Inevitably she saw him. *Costas.* His wide-shouldered frame and smouldering eyes filled her mind as always.

There was no escape, even though they worked hard to avoid each other. He haunted her waking hours as well as her sleep—an edgy, demanding presence that she craved, despite her efforts to be sensible.

He was pure temptation. He couldn't give her what she longed for and she couldn't settle for the little he offered. But the strain of resisting him was almost unbearable.

Especially when he'd tried to make amends. Not just with easy things like the bouquet of ice-white roses and a written apology after their confrontation. Or the offer of an Aegean island tour on his yacht, no strings attached.

No, what she appreciated was far more intangible. The first time she'd visited her grandfather she'd left feeling hollowed out, shocked by the depth of her inner turmoil. She'd emerged from the room to find Costas waiting. Tall, silent and surprisingly comforting. She hadn't even objected when his hand, hard and hot, encircled her elbow and he wordlessly led her away.

They'd walked in silence through the hospital. Costas' expression had been unreadable. But something about his taut features as he'd looked back at her spoke of understanding. Strength and sympathy.

Ever since, whenever she left her grandfather, Costas was waiting. And his solid presence, his unquestioning support, meant more than she'd thought possible.

Sophie opened her eyes, determined to clear it of his disturbing presence. She turned and headed down the steep track to the cove below the Palamidis villa.

There were so many thoughts and fears crowding her mind: Eleni's progress; her feelings for her grandfather; and the dilemma of when to go home. It was time to pick up her life in Sydney. But somehow she couldn't make the decision to leave.

She'd told herself she stayed for Eleni. She'd come to care for her and knew the little girl loved having her around. She refused to dwell on the possibility that it was because of her likeness to Eleni's mother.

Then too, she wanted to explore the tenuous bond with Petros Liakos. She'd told him she must leave soon and he'd welcomed her idea that she return for another visit to Crete.

But above all there was Costas. The man tied her emotions in knots and her mind into a syrupy pulp of yearning. And her body—hell! He only had to come close and all pretence of control left her. It was as if something in her body, and in her soul, came alive only when she was with him.

The light was almost gone when she reached the beach, but the sand was still warm and inviting. She dropped to her knees as the emotions she'd tried so hard to suppress bubbled up.

How she missed her mum! How much she needed her love and guidance. She'd give anything to wake up and find her mother's death had been a nightmare. If only the doctors had diagnosed the illness sooner. If only her mother had listened to her when Sophie had told her to rest. If only the drugs had worked. If only…

Her head and shoulders bowed. She pressed her hands to her eyes, feeling the wetness there as tears streamed down her cheeks. Her mouth slackened, lips quivering till the sobs welled up from deep inside her and she gave in to the force of her grief.

It was dark when she finally raised her head, bereft now of tears. Evening had fallen, like the sudden drop of a curtain. But early stars already bloomed.

The storm of weeping had left her boneless, curiously empty as she huddled there. Eventually she braced her hands on the ground to lever herself up. But her right hand didn't touch sand. It fastened on something soft.

In the gloom she could make out the large, pale shape beside her. A towel.

Clutching the cotton towelling with both hands, she stumbled to her feet, then swayed as the circulation returning to her legs prickled her.

This was a private estate with high-tech security. No tourists allowed here. She turned and stared out into the cove. She'd have seen anyone swimming when she arrived. Wouldn't she? Or had she been too caught up in her own miserable thoughts to notice the quiet stroke of a swimmer? There'd been no one in the shallows. But further out…?

The steady shush of waves on the shore was loud in her ears, she couldn't hear anything else. But then she became aware of movement. A black shape in the sea. It headed straight in to the beach. And now she could make out the faint echo of sound, the splash of a body forging its way through the velvet dark water.

Her eyes had become accustomed to the darkness and she saw the precise moment he reached the shallows and found his footing. His wide, rangy shoulders emerged and he shook his head. Water sluiced, streaming over his massive chest, broad and heavy, down his narrowing torso to a lean waist.

And yet Sophie couldn't look away. Her breath snared somewhere in her chest as she watched Costas—it could be no one else—rise from the lapping waves.

She should call out, warn him that he wasn't alone.

She should turn her back, give him the privacy she'd demand herself.

For even in the deep gloom of early evening she could see that he was nude. No shadow of a swimsuit marred the perfect, athletic lines of his body.

Her breathing faltered, even her pulse stuttered as she stared, transfixed.

He was perfect. Every taut, ultra-masculine inch of him.

He'd seen her. He stopped in mid-stride, still knee-deep in water.
Go. Now!
Drop the towel and disappear as fast as you can.

Her mind screamed at her to run. To take herself off before it was too late. They'd been through this before—the searing physical attraction, the driving need.

It was all he wanted, all he needed from her. He'd never offer her anything more.

Sophie swallowed hard, trying to summon the strength to ignore the potency of her response to him, her own needs. The longer she stood, transfixed by his presence, the weaker grew the voice of self-preservation. Till it became only a blur of white noise buzzing in her ears.

Out of the morass of painful emotion, out of the guilt and grief and doubt, only one thing was absolutely clear to her. How much she wanted this man. Wanted him body and soul. Needed him with a desperation that was beyond understanding. Beyond right and wrong or fear for the future.

She remembered the bliss of his mouth on hers, his hands on her body, his heat against her own. And she wanted that again.

This craving for comfort, *for Costas,* was self-destructive. Foolish. But right now it was beyond her to do anything but stand and wait for him.

She'd been strong for so long. She just couldn't do it any more.

'Sophie.' His voice was as hypnotic as the susurrating waves.

He strode forward till he stood on dry land. Starlight limned the well-defined ridges and curves of his muscled body. The stark angle of his jaw. The bunch of his fists. The heavy fullness of his muscled thighs. His complete maleness.

Sophie gripped the towel tighter in her clenched fingers, feeling the now familiar burst of heat ignite within her. She was trembling hard as she stared back at him unable, unwilling, to look away.

'Sophie.' Her name on his lips was a groan this time, long and low and pained. 'Go away.'

She knew he was right. That in the bright light of day she'd run a mile from the dangerous undercurrents swirling around them.

But, heaven help her, she couldn't fight any more. All she felt was need. Pure, driving need. Nothing else mattered. Not the memory of his brutal words when they'd kissed, nor the pain she'd felt afterwards. She'd lived with loss and hurt so long now that she didn't care about tomorrow. Didn't care about anything but the extraordinary completeness she felt only with him.

He stalked up the beach, silent and sure-footed. Sophie swallowed hard, trembling at his aura of potent energy. He looked bigger than ever. Impossibly masculine and exciting. Some atavistic part of her wanted to flee before him—the embodiment of the primitive, dangerous male hunter.

She could smell the heady scent of musk on his wet skin and wondered how it would taste to her tongue.

Just that wayward thought sent her temperature soaring.

'Don't you hear me?' he growled. 'Go back to the house.'

He was so close she could feel his hot breath against her face and tilted her chin up towards it, closing her eyes. Even straight from the icy Aegean, his skin burned like a furnace. She could feel the heat of his bare flesh.

His breathing sawed heavy and stertorous, louder even than her galloping pulse.

'Sto Diavolo.' His voice was a hoarse rasp of despair. 'You would try the patience of a saint! Don't you have any sense at all?' He sounded desperate.

He couldn't be any more desperate than she.

She swayed towards the sound of his voice and his hands clamped on her shoulders, sure and possessive. She sighed at the thrill of anticipation that shot down through her arms, her torso, at his touch. Her nipples peaked in immediate, agonising sensitivity.

'No, Sophie.' Costas' voice rumbled from above her. 'No, we can't.'

But his fingers spread over her shoulders, surreptitiously massaging an erotic message into her flesh. His body communicated directly to hers, and there was no mistaking his intent, despite his verbal denial.

She lifted her hand, reaching out till she felt his chilled, wet, burning flesh beneath the pads of her fingers.

His breath hissed violently as his hands spasmed tight then splayed wide over her shoulders.

Slowly, deliberately, she planted her whole hand against him, skin to skin, and a world of sensation exploded across her palm. She traced the solid ridge of his collar bone, paused at the clavicle and rose to the pulse point beneath his jaw. The life blood throbbed violently there. It raced in a frenzied tattoo that echoed her own heartbeat thudding so hard against her ribcage.

'You mustn't touch—ahh!' His words died as she let her hand slide down over the firm strength of his broad chest, finding the crisp, enticing silk of hair, the thud of his heart hammering deep inside.

His hands slipped then, from her shoulders to her arms, round her back, returning to her neck, her face, pushing into her hair and holding her still.

His kiss was ruthless—his mouth urgent and hard. His tongue aggressively proprietorial as it explored, dominated, demanded her unstinting response.

If she'd had any shred of will-power left to resist him it would have melted at the first erotic, knowing lap of his tongue against hers. At the sensation of his searing breath filling her mouth.

She wrapped her arms tight round his wet torso, pulling herself flush against his blazing heat, his slick flesh. Feeling his solid, un-yielding muscles against her skin. His erection pressed long and hard against her. His thighs braced wide enough to encompass her.

It was so exactly *right*. Instinctively Sophie knew this was what she'd wanted from the very first. She and Costas together. That was what she'd craved. What she'd pushed into a dark corner of her consciousness, as if she could hide it away!

The surge of possessiveness that filled her numbed brain was so strong it rocked her. It was even more powerful than the pulsing, urgent need, the wild yearning for more. More sensation. More feeling. More…

'Sophie.' She felt rather than heard him speak her name between their frantic kisses. The sensation of his deep voice thrumming through her, hoarse with passion as he groaned out her name, erased the last tiny vestige of fear that it might be Fotini he was thinking of.

Costas was with *her,* truly wanted *her.*

And there was no doubt in her mind they belonged together.

'Tell me to stop, Sophie.'

How could she send him away when his kisses set her on fire? When his body beckoned hers with such irresistible promise and shivered in response at the very touch of her hands? How could she send him away when he was hers?

Whatever logic said, or the law, or cold common sense, Sophie recognised it now with absolute certainly. Costas was *hers.* This was right.

She sighed into his mouth. This was perfect.

* * *

Costas heard her sigh. Felt it in her warm, fresh breath mingling with his own. Tasted it, sweet and conquering, deep in his mouth.

And he knew he was lost.

He let his hands slide from her silky hair, rove her delicately moulded body as he'd longed to ever since he'd seen her standing there, waiting for him in the twilight.

He'd thought he was seeing things. An apparition come to seduce his waking mind just as she'd come to him every night in his tortured erotic dreams.

But she was real. He lashed his arms tight round her, pulling her against him, imprinting every gorgeous, seductive centimetre of her body against his. She felt too good to be true. Too perfect.

Like Circe, the sorceress who enslaved men with her magical beauty.

No woman had ever been this perfect. Ever.

He shuddered as she smoothed her hands down his back, into the curve at the base of his spine and out, fingers edging over his buttocks.

Instantly his whirling half-formed thoughts blacked out. He was incapable of thinking coherently now. Instead it was instinct that drove him. He kissed her so comprehensively that she bowed back over his arm. Tucked her lower body in against him.

He moved automatically, taking her down with him as he knelt, finding the beach towel with one hand and shaking it out to spread on the sand.

He didn't even break their kiss as he prevented her automatic movement to lie down. Her breath still seared into his mouth as he worked the buttons on her shirt undone, dragged her hands away from him so he could strip the top from her. The bra took only a single, tearing wrench and then his hands found her breasts. Firm, pouting, ripe breasts that she pushed into his palms as she sighed her delight into his mouth.

Oh, lord. He was going to die. She was killing him.

He was never going to restrain himself. Even as he fondled the soft, tantalising fullness of her, palmed and squeezed her hard nipples, his whole being focused on the effort it took *not* simply to strip away her jeans and thrust himself into her like some marauding barbarian.

She pulled away, stunning him with the loss of her soft warmth. Instinctively he followed, finding himself on all fours as she lay back on the towel. Her eyes were unreadable in this light but they were fixed on him.

His heart gave a single, enormous thump that juddered through him.

Then his eyes dropped to her hands, busy tugging down her jeans. Her panties. Revealing a dark triangle of femininity. The tender curve of rounded hips. Slim, shapely thighs.

He'd reach out to help her pull the denim from her legs but he didn't dare. If he touched her…

He shut his eyes, summoning desperate control. Willing himself to exercise some restraint.

But even in the dark he could see her naked before him. Feel again the impossibly soft texture of her breasts filling his hands. Taste her, warm and generous, in his mouth.

Their breathing was loud in his ears. That and the thud of his racing pulse.

He braced himself. Even the sound of her uneven gasps was seductive music to his bewitched senses.

And the scent of her. The fresh, always enticing perfume of her. It was overlaid now with a tangy, musky invitation. Female scent. His nostrils flared and his arms, braced hard against the ground, trembled.

'Costas.' It was the merest sigh of sound. And yet it was charged with the same need that drove him.

He opened his eyes to the woman lying before him. She reached out one slim arm and he felt her fingers trail across his chest.

He surged over her. Covering her completely so that the magic sensation of her warm, soft female flesh greeted him, tantalised him even more.

His breath was expelled in a huge sigh. The fit of their bodies was magnificent. Mind-numbing.

She moved her legs, shifting them outwards so that he felt the smooth skin of her thighs against the outer edges of his own. He let her take just a little more of his weight, allowing his lower body to sink against the feminine core of her.

There was a hiss of breath, his or hers he didn't know. And movement. Friction, deliberate invitation. Had she lifted her hips or had he thrust against her?

He was too dazed by the onslaught against his senses to be sure. All he knew was that he had to concentrate on not moving. Not doing anything. Just till he—

She shifted her legs, sliding her thighs up and around his, encircling him. She reached up, linking her arms round his neck, tugging him down. And of course he went, leaning into her, kissing her feverishly, knowing he could never get enough of her.

The more he got the more he wanted. He was a doomed man.

He drew back slightly, brushing his hand lightly across the juncture of her thighs, slowing to explore the delicate folds there.

Sophie moaned into his mouth and the blood rushed faster in his arteries. The tension in him so immense he trembled with it.

There. His questing fingers struck gold and her whole body jolted. And again.

And then she was urging him nearer. Her legs tight round him, her hands clutching him, her lips fretful against his.

No man could withstand the temptation.

He pressed forward, found her slick and welcoming, pulling him closer, deeper, further. Then with a single uncontrollable thrust he joined them so completely that there was no ending and no beginning.

The shocked, shattering silence held for just a second and then he felt Sophie tremble in his arms. From the inside out it started, until the trembling became her shuddering, rocking climax. And the inevitable, answering motion began in him, so that he withdrew then pushed even further, tighter, faster into her. Till the world shattered in a blur of roaring flames and dazzling light.

CHAPTER TWELVE

ECSTASY.

That was what this was, Costas thought dazedly as he wrapped Sophie against him. Starlight silvered her lithe curves as she sprawled across him—a living, breathing, sensuous blanket.

He knew he should take time to assess the situation, engage his brain. Something nagged at him, some hint of trouble.

His conscience? He should be appalled that he hadn't found the strength to push her away.

The litany of reasons he shouldn't get involved with her: her strained emotional state, her status as a guest and as Eleni's relative and benefactress…the taboos had crumbled to dust when he'd found her waiting for him on the shore.

She'd been pure seduction. Inviting him. Enticing him. *Wanting* him—as much, it seemed, as he wanted her.

He should have resisted, should have been strong for both of them, but it had been impossible.

And there was no turning back now. No help for her, or him, once that first barrier had been breached. One touch and his control had vanished.

And, the good lord help him, he could think of nothing but how miraculous it had been. How miraculous Sophie was. His instinct had been right. They were explosive together. Sex had never been so earth-shattering.

He dropped a leaden hand to the soft spread of her hair across her shoulder.

Mine. All mine.

At least for tonight, he hastily reminded himself. That was all he wanted, all he needed—a night of bliss to counteract the burden of his days.

But was that enough?

He frowned and his hold on her tightened a fraction. She murmured, her warm breath hazing the hollow of his neck and he froze, stunned to discover his body wasn't quite as sated as he'd thought.

He smoothed his hand over her bare skin, savouring the delicious sensation, and his mouth curved into a smile so wide it felt as if it might split his cheeks. Anticipation hummed in his blood.

The night was still young.

He had her now—exactly as he'd imagined so many times. She'd come to him at last, of her own volition, made it clear she understood and accepted his terms. Sex, physical release, comfort—exactly what they both needed.

And it had been worth the wait.

He felt alive again. More alive than he'd felt in years. Than he'd ever felt.

No wonder lightning crackled in the air whenever they were together. The sensual charge between them was unbelievable. Unique. And that made for mind-blowing sex.

His grin grew impossibly wider.

He felt as if he'd been through cataclysm and fire. Death and rebirth. His very bones had dissolved in the intensity of their passion.

But now he was looking forward to the next time. He stroked a hand over her back. She was exhausted. Sleeping. It wouldn't be right to disturb her. Not yet.

But she was getting cold, he realised as he felt goose-pimples on her shoulder. He had no idea how long they'd been lying here in each other's arms, but the night was cooling.

Time to get his lover inside.

This time he knew his grin was smug. The thought of Sophie in his bed, where the lamplight would illuminate each glowing centimetre of her body and reveal every nuance of her response to him…

It was the work of a moment to wrap her in the towel and hoist her into his arms. He strode towards the track up to the house, grateful for the starlight to guide him.

'Costas?' The word feathered across his bare chest, low and tentative.

'Just relax,' he murmured. 'I've got you.'

And I'm not going to let you go.

Even carrying her in his arms came naturally, as if she were designed precisely for him.

'Our clothes—'

'Are safe where they are.'

She was silent a moment and then he felt her palm against his chest, hot like a brand.

'No. I need to get my clothes. I—'

'They're unimportant, *glikia mou.* You won't need them again tonight.' The words heightened the anticipation already humming through his taut frame. He lengthened his stride.

'No!'

His pace faltered at her vehement denial.

'No,' she repeated. 'Someone might see.'

He laughed, relief lightening the sudden tension in his chest. For an instant he'd thought she meant to deny him. 'No need to worry, Sophie. I have my own private entrance. The servants know not to intrude on my privacy unless told to.'

Her hair teased his flesh as she shook her head. Her hand pushed harder against him.

'No! I don't want…' She paused. 'Put me down.'

'No need for that.' He hugged her tight. Revelling in the smooth softness of her body against his where the towel had slipped. 'I know this path like the back of my hand. You don't.'

Already they'd reached the olive grove, a shadowed glade where the darkness was thicker.

'I *said* put me down!' The rapid rise and fall of her breasts told him as much as her words. He stopped, barely preventing an impatient sigh.

Why did women have to get so hung up about inessentials?

Hadn't he already promised no one but he would see her? And she couldn't be worried about a pair of jeans! No one was going to steal them.

'Please.'

He could resist her, barely, when she argued with him, when she fought and challenged and defied him. But when she whispered in that low, honey-sweet voice, he had no defence.

He shifted his hold, trying and failing abysmally to ignore the sensation of her bare skin against him. There was minuscule comfort in the sound of her indrawn hiss of breath, telling him she felt the same excitement that held him rigid.

Slowly he lowered her, deliberately letting her slide centimetre by centimetre down his body. The towel dropped away, leaving only the two of them, naked flesh to naked flesh, on fire again with the most primitive of needs.

Blood pulsed loud in his ears, a counterpoint to their ragged breathing. Sweat broke across his skin as he felt her silken body press intimately against him.

Maybe stopping here in the olive grove wasn't such a bad idea. The grass was long and soft, still scented with the day's perfume of wild flowers.

He splayed his hands over her back, down, down, to cup her buttocks and draw her close against him. She shuddered, her hands tightening her hold on his shoulders.

He grinned into her hair.

No, stopping here wasn't a bad idea at all.

Sophie caught her breath on a sigh of abandonment. Of raw pleasure.

Why did Costas' touch excite her so? The feel of his gaze on her? The awareness that they were alone, naked and wanting?

She'd felt desire before. Had some limited experience of it before Costas Palamidis had erupted into her life.

She thought she'd known...

Sophie shook her head. She'd known nothing.

She swallowed a moan of pure pleasure as his big hands

swiped low over her body, pulling her close to his flagrant, heavy erection. The sensation was exquisite.

It seemed only a few minutes ago that they'd had each other, consumed by a need so long repressed it had been combustible.

Yet already he wanted her again. As she did him.

Surely now he recognised it too—the remarkable *rightness* of them together. It was physical desire but it was so much more too. She felt it deep in her very soul.

Something wonderful had happened between them.

Despite the tension drawing heavily at every muscle, her mouth curved up in a smile that grazed the damp skin of his chest. She tasted the salty tang of him on her lips.

There was something heady, something exciting, about having all that raw male power, all that potent energy focused on her. She could get used to—

'Sophie.' His voice was a throaty rumble in her ear as he bent to press his lips to her neck, feather-light kisses up past her jawbone. The tug of his teeth against her ear lobe had her knees buckling and it was only his arms wrapped round her, the strength of him supporting her, that stopped her from falling.

And then she *was* falling. Gently tugged off balance, to tumble forward and land sprawled against him as he lay back on the grass. Her heart raced as she recognised the scent of desire in the air. Her breasts were crushed against his massive chest so she felt the rapid thump of his heart beating time with hers. His hands slid over her, fast, restless, hungry.

And Sophie knew the hunger that had woken in her at the sight of him emerging from the sea hadn't been assuaged at all. The yearning for completion, for fulfilment was far stronger now than before.

Then she hadn't known how it could be. Now she did and she craved it with every cell in her body. That sense of sharing, of bonding, had been so complete it was pure ecstasy.

'Kiss me,' he demanded, dragging her up the length of him. His glorious, hard, aroused body lay beneath her. The friction of flesh against flesh, of teasing body hair against smooth skin, made her gasp. And when he pulled her head down to his, it was for an erotic kiss, tongue laving tongue.

He tasted like every dream come true. Potent and strong and sensuously, darkly sweet. Sophie cupped his face in her hands, loving the slightly abrasive temptation of his jaw, the hint of a tremor in his hard hands as she kissed him back.

'Yes!' The single sibilant word hissed in her ear as she moved to kiss his chin, his cheek, nuzzle his neck, nip at the sensitive flesh of his ear.

Costas' hands slid down, shaping the indent of her waist, slowing at the curve of her hips, grasping her bottom and pulling her against him, hard and blatant in his need for her. Against her ear he whispered a stream of Greek, of words she barely registered. But she understood enough to know he was describing her power over him, his need for her, and exactly what he wanted to do with her.

His voice was the most exciting thing she'd ever heard, urging her on as his hands tightened on her hips, his thighs nudged hers wider, till she felt soft meadow grass beneath her knees. And at the centre of her was him.

He waited. Let her choose her own pace. Only his deep voice, throbbing low and sensuous in her ear, his hands clamped possessively on her hips, told her of the urgency of his need. And the feel of him, hot and hard beneath her.

She levered herself up with her hands on the ground near his shoulders. She gasped as he took her breasts in his hands, petting them gently, then not gently at all, till she cried out at the exquisite delight that shuddered through her, so close to yet so different to pain.

And then he was suckling her. He made her squirm against him, her head thrown back so she could gulp down shuddering breaths of meadow-scented air.

'I can't get enough of you, Sophie,' he murmured against her breast. 'Never enough. You make me burn like I've never burned before.'

She looked down at his dark sculpted face, strong even in the deep shadows. Saw him take her nipple in his mouth, felt the sweet pang of delight spear through her, and felt the trembling begin in every part of her body.

It was the sight of him. The feel of him. But more, there was something else, some powerful connection that drew her to him, linked her invisibly but inexorably to him. That met his need with answering need, desire with desire. And melted the brittle barrier of icy grief around her heart.

Emotion swelled within her. She wanted to cradle him, hold him, pleasure him.

Love him.

She felt protective, possessive and more turned on than she'd ever been in her life.

'Costas…' She needed to tell him, make him understand how she felt. This was so momentous, so extraordinary.

Then he was kissing her, plundering her mouth with a raw hunger that sent fire shimmering through her veins, urgency pounding in her brain.

It took all her strength to break their kiss and draw back. He lay below her, dark eyes fixed on her, his massive chest heaving. As desperate, as wanting as she was.

Sophie reached down to slide her fingers round him. Her eyes widened as she realised just how well-endowed he was. He'd felt stupendous before, but now…

His hiss of indrawn breath was loud in the stillness. 'Don't, Sophie!'

The power she felt was exciting. She was heady with it. He throbbed in her hands and something clenched deep inside her. The sight of Costas, obviously at the edge of his control, was intoxicating.

'Why? Don't you like it?'

For answer his hands cupped her bottom and he pulled her closer, until all thought of games fled her mind and there was only need. His hands were urgent, his body thrust against her and she sighed at how good he felt.

'Do it!' he growled, his voice hoarse. 'Now!' He lifted her up, urging her against him.

For a moment she strained, poised above him, delighting in the sensation of him watching her with hooded eyes, knowing he was as excited by the sight and feel of her as she was by him.

And then she couldn't wait any longer. She sank down slowly. Deep inside she felt him. Tighter, fuller, impossibly more than even the last time.

'Costas?' Her voice trembled with doubt.

'Sh, *Sophie mou*. It's all right,' he whispered. 'I'll make it all right.'

And he did. His hands swept over her, came up to cup her breasts, squeezing gently in a way that loosened every tensing muscle in her body. And from beneath her he pushed up steadily, deliberately, creating waves of erotic sensation that swamped her senses.

His rhythm increased and automatically she matched it, rising and falling against him in a quickening pace that pounded relentlessly in her blood. She felt the muscle-packed strength of him beneath her, surging into her. The callus-hard caress of his hands on her. The sound of his breathing, as laboured as her own. And his eyes. She felt their heat on her as she moved above him.

She felt like a queen. Powerful, commanding. She felt…

Her breath snagged as the surge of sensation caught her suddenly, overpoweringly. Each movement was exquisite torture, pushing her higher and closer. She grabbed for Costas, her hands grasping his wrists as he held her breasts. He bucked up harder against her, the heavy weight of his thighs pure power against her legs.

And then she exploded. Reality came apart in one shattering, shuddering moment that rolled on and on, prolonged by the insistent rhythm of his body.

When at last the sensations eased he pulled her down hard against him, expelling her breath with his force.

She lay over him, his heart throbbing beneath her, his hot breath riffling her hair, his body so powerfully alive beneath her, within her. The smoky musk aroma of aroused male filled her nostrils. His arms wrapped tight round her as if he'd never let her go. Even when she felt his tempo increase to fever pitch, he held her close. He pulsed, warm and throbbing within her, exciting her with a primitive satisfaction.

Suddenly, out of nowhere, the tension spiralled in her again, drawing her with him into a shared experience of fulfilment.

They were so close they were one. His climax was hers. His body belonged to her. *He* was hers.

She loved him, she realised.

She loved Costas Vassilis Palamidis. The arrogant, caring, tender, proud man who'd taken over her life in every way.

Should she feel shock? Disbelief?

Drowsily Sophie smiled, delighting in the feel of his hot, silky skin against her lips. She didn't feel anything right now except a sense of rightness.

Bliss.

Sophie half opened her eyes and protested. Costas still held her close, his heart beating steadily beneath her, his arms holding her. She wanted to snuggle in against him, stay like this forever, but something had changed.

She had it now, the steady rhythm that lulled her, kept her in a lazy haze of well-being. It was the feel of him striding, cradling her in his arms.

She fought to lift her eyelids, to check where they were. There was a light somewhere, making her slit her heavy lids against its brightness. He shifted his hold, pressing her face in against his collar-bone, where she caught the salt scent of the sea and man. Drowsily she pressed her open lips against his skin, loving the tangy taste against her tongue.

He shuddered, holding her tighter till she was consumed by the sense of him all around her. He muttered something she couldn't catch.

Then there was a sudden whooshing sound behind her, making her blink her eyes wide open.

They were in a room, the lights concealed around the rim of the ceiling as she looked over his shoulder.

A bathroom, a massive bathroom, warm with the glow of

rosy tinted marble, glittering from the light reflecting off enormous mirrors and gold fittings.

'Shower with me, Sophie.' His voice rumbled beneath her ear. He leaned forward and she felt a haze of warm spray sprinkle her shoulder.

That woke her from her lethargy. She opened her eyes wide, staring straight into Costas' gaze. This time she had no trouble reading his thoughts. Mischief danced in his black eyes just as surely as it curved his strong, sensuous mouth in a smile that stole her breath.

Her heart seemed to swell as she stared back, mesmerised by his male beauty, and by sheer delight.

It was too much.

These feelings, the wondrous knowledge of this new emotional bond between them, of love…it was too much. Surely her heart would burst out of her ribcage.

She loved him so. Adored him. Even down to the smug anticipation lighting his expression.

He was definitely a man with but one thing on his mind. She took in his expression. Lust. Anticipation.

Out of nowhere fear jagged through her brain. Remembered pain.

Her body tensed as insidious doubt wormed its way into her brain. Could she be wrong? Was it possible she'd made a mistake? That his passion was, after all, only skin-deep? As shallow as a simple desire for a bed partner.

Could it be that he hadn't experienced the revelation she had?

Goose-pimples rose on her arms as a sudden chill encompassed her.

As she watched, his smile faded. His face grew serious, as if he could read her doubt and fear.

'Sophie,' he murmured. 'You're like a light in the darkness.' His voice was hoarse with emotion. A mirror to her own overwhelming feelings. His eyes held the same wonder. 'I can't imagine what I've done to deserve you.'

He leaned down, pressed a lingering, tender kiss against her lips.

Sophie shut her eyes, knowing that here, in his arms, she'd come home. She hadn't made some terrible mistake.

This was where she was meant to be.

Hungry for his caresses, even more for his love, she linked her arms up round his neck, tugging him to her.

The kiss escalated from gentle to lush. From lush to languorously seductive. And then to passionate. Desperate.

It only ended when he stepped into a huge shower compartment and warm jets of water sprayed across them.

'You can put me down,' she spluttered, wiping a lock of wet hair back from her face.

He did, lowering her slowly to her feet, and then keeping his hands on her arms, holding her steady as she swayed.

She watched the water sluice down, plastering his dark hair to his head, glistening on every curve and angle of his hard chest, highlighting every masculine plane and curve. She sucked in her breath on a sigh of sheer wonder.

Costas lifted a hand and smoothed her hair back over her shoulder, his hand lingering to curve around her neck, splay-fingered in a possessive hold.

Sophie couldn't stop the smile that shaped her lips as she leaned close to his touch. She was acting on instinct and instinct told her this was the most wonderful experience of her life.

He stepped closer, reaching round behind her then holding out a cake of soap in his hand.

'I've been wanting to do this ever since the first time I saw you,' he said, his voice husky.

She remembered him that first day. All soaking-wet muscle and barely suppressed impatience as he'd forced her under the shower. Even then, sick and grief-stricken, she'd barely been able to take her eyes off his magnificent body.

And now…she had the right to do more than look.

Mesmerised, she watched him lather the soap between his hands, slowly, methodically, and then reach behind her to put it down. His breath was warm against her face as his hands, slippery with soap bubbles, skimmed across her collar-bone, down the curve to her breasts, where he slowed and circled, till she bit down on her lip to stop from calling out. She reached for his shoulders, needing his strength to stay upright as the slow, erotic swirl of his hands weakened her knees.

'There are so many things I've been wanting to do with you, Sophie.' His voice was a low rumble and his smile was taut as his hands smoothed a path down her ribcage, into the indentation of her waist, out across the flare of her hips and then lower.

CHAPTER THIRTEEN

SOPHIE NEVER WANTED to move. She could stay like this forever.

She was sprawled in the largest, most luxurious bed she'd ever seen. The rich cotton sheets were soft against her skin. Her body felt light, almost weightless, but at the same time ultra-sensitive, after hour upon hour of lovemaking.

Even now she felt a warm curl of satisfaction deep in her belly at how well-loved she'd been.

No wonder she didn't have the strength yet to raise her head or open her eyes.

Last night Costas had been so voracious in his need for her. Under his tutelage she'd responded uninhibitedly. They'd taken each other to peak after peak, as desire was rekindled time and again.

He'd been boldly demanding. Outrageously seductive. Fiercely passionate. And incredibly tender.

He'd brought tears to her eyes more than once. And the way he'd watched her so intensely, refusing to turn out the light precisely, he said, because he needed to see her. She shivered, remembering the intensity of his regard. At first she'd been reluctant, preferring to hide her responses to him. But then she'd discovered just what he meant, as she watched him lose control for her. Just for her.

That was the reason she felt so good.

It wasn't just the sex. It was the bond, so strong now between them that she *knew* he felt it just as much as she did.

Maybe this time when he woke there'd be time for conversation, for declarations.

She wriggled, snuggling down beneath the sheet.

It took her a while to realise that for the first time since she'd seen Costas stalking out of the sea towards her, she couldn't feel him. All night he'd been close, touching, embracing, stroking. Teasing. As if he couldn't bear her as far as arm's length from him.

Which had suited her just fine.

Sophie swiped her foot across the bed.

Nothing.

She frowned and dragged her hand across the sheet till her arm stretched across the centre of the mattress.

It was cold.

She frowned. The bathroom? She couldn't hear anything. But the rooms were soundproofed. Heat scorched her throat and cheeks as she remembered Costas reassuring her last night that she could be as loud as she liked and no one but he could hear.

She opened her eyes and saw it was morning. Not only that—it was late. The glare of full sun rimmed the curtains. She rolled onto her back and found herself alone.

A cold weight settled in her stomach, pressing down.

Ridiculous. There was nothing wrong. Costas was probably in the shower, maybe even waiting for her.

She threw back the sheet and crawled to the end of the bed, aware now of the dull, delicious ache of muscles rarely used. She was a little self-conscious by the time she reached the door to the *en suite* bathroom. But that was ridiculous. After all that had happened between them there was no need to be.

Nevertheless she paused and knocked.

No answer.

She rapped harder with her knuckles, waited for the door to swing open and Costas to smile down at her, his eyes glittering with secret promise.

Eventually she opened the door and walked in. The bathroom was empty.

Again she felt that heavy, plunging sensation in her stomach.

Not foreboding. Just a need for food. She'd have it as soon as Costas returned. He'd probably gone onto the balcony for some fresh air.

Sophie crossed to the bedroom window and opened the curtain enough to see the large balcony. It was empty too. She repressed a frown. He'd gone downstairs to get some food for them. That was all.

She swung away and turned towards the bed. And stopped.

On the floor beside where she'd lain was a neat pile of clothes.

Slowly she paced towards it, recognising a T-shirt and a pair of jeans that had just been washed—they'd only been put in her wardrobe yesterday. Undies, bra, even a pair of flat-heeled sandals and her hairbrush.

Suddenly Sophie found herself sitting in a club chair near the bed. These weren't the clothes she'd worn yesterday. Costas had dressed, gone to her room and found something for her to wear then left the bundle by the bed. All without bothering to wake her.

What sort of message was that?

Blankly she stared, trying to work out what had happened. Trying so hard not to jump to conclusions. She wasn't well-acquainted with the rules for dealing with the morning after.

But then she hadn't thought of this as a *morning after*. She'd been so sure it was a new beginning. Not an ending.

She sucked in a breath, holding her palm against her ribs where a stitch caught her. A dull ache started up somewhere deep inside.

Eventually she moved. Took her time showering, dressing, brushing out her knotted hair. All the while waiting for the sound of a door slamming open, the quick, decisive stride she'd come to know so well. The deep, sensuous voice that had urged her to ecstasy.

Costas' room remained stubbornly empty. As was hers. As was the whole upper floor.

He's gone to the hospital, she told herself. That must be it.

Anxiety bloomed in the pit of her stomach. Had Eleni taken a turn for the worse? Was there a crisis?

She shook her head, striving to control her breathing. No. If it was serious Costas would have told her, or left word. She knew he would have.

So why hadn't he woken her? Told her he had to leave? Or even scribbled a note? Why leave her to wake alone and wondering?

She frowned as she stared at her watch. It wasn't breakfast she'd missed. It was lunch too. She'd been so exhausted she'd slept more solidly than she had in weeks.

Which meant Costas had probably been gone for hours.

By the time she descended to the ground floor Sophie felt unseasonably chilled, as if the cold had gone bone-deep despite the bright sunshine outside.

No one in the dining room, or the sitting room, or—

'*Kalimera, thespinis.*'

Sophie swung round to see the housekeeper emerge from the servants' quarters.

'*Kalimera sas,*' she responded, her smile shaky.

'You have slept well, yes? Would you like some food?'

'I'll wait, thanks,' she said. '*Kyrie Palamidis* and I had some things to discuss. I'll wait and eat with him.'

The housekeeper tilted her head, her expression puzzled.

'But the *kyrios* left the house hours ago,' she explained. 'He visited the hospital first. Then he rang to say he'd decided to take some business meetings. He won't be back until this evening. You take a seat and I'll bring you a nice meal, in just a few minutes.' She smiled and nodded and turned back the way she'd come.

Which was just as well. Otherwise she'd have known something was terribly wrong when Sophie stumbled blindly to a hard-backed chair and collapsed onto it.

One shuddering breath. Another.

Sophie forced the air down into her lungs. She felt the excruciating stab of pain straight to her heart.

She knew now why Costas had slipped away. And stayed away all day. As far as he was concerned nothing had changed. And there was nothing more to be said between them.

Sex. That's what I want. That's all I want.

She slammed her hands over her ears but nothing could stop the hateful memory of those words echoing in her head.

I want to forget the world for a single night. Sex and ecstasy and animal pleasure.

Scalding tears welled in her eyes as she remembered how ferociously he'd responded to her last night. Just how much *animal pleasure* he drawn from her willing body through the long hours of darkness.

When she'd stupidly thought they were making love.

No relationship. No future.

The words were a death knell to her fragile hopes.

She'd been a fool last night, carried away by the strength of her need. By her *love* for him.

Stupidly she'd believed that because she felt far more than lust, Costas must now too. But nothing had changed for him.

She choked back the bitter taste of despair.

She knew exactly where she stood with Costas Palamidis.

CHAPTER FOURTEEN

COSTAS MANOEUVRED THE car around another swooping curve on the road home. He kept the powerful engine at a moderate speed, unwilling to follow his inclination and floor the accelerator. There was no need to hurry, he assured himself. That would be a sign of weakness.

He was a man who'd always prided himself on his strength of character. And he would not weaken now. No matter how great the incentive.

But he permitted himself a smile at the thought of the delicious temptation awaiting him at home.

Sophie.

Generous and ripely seductive. A revelation even to a man of his experience. Never had he possessed a lover who turned night into glorious, dazzling day for him. Who made his blood sing and his senses swim. Who stripped him bare of all civilised refinement and reduced him to mindless ecstasy.

Was it any wonder he'd been careful to keep his distance today?

A man needed to retain some control, some perspective. He couldn't allow a love affair, however delightful, to cloud his judgement. He had responsibilities. A daughter to care for. A multinational business to direct.

No. He needed to remember that a lover could not be permitted to take over his life.

He'd woken to the pearly dawn light and to a sense of such

fulfilment, such peace and such fizzing anticipation, that it alarmed him.

Hell, it had *terrified* him! He could admit that to himself at least.

He'd felt the smooth curve of Sophie's waist beneath his palm, smelt the love-scent of her, heady in his nostrils, and knew he never wanted to leave her.

Hell! What sort of nonsense was that?

An illusion left over from the starlight when she'd come to him like a goddess out of the darkness. When she'd been the lover he'd yearned for. Absolute perfection.

He shook his head, to clear it of the fantasy that even now clouded his thinking.

She'd played havoc with his thought processes. With his self-control. For a while there she'd even tempted him into thinking he needed more from her. Something other than sexual satisfaction and the blissful, mindless release it brought.

The woman was too dangerous.

So he'd left her. A tactical withdrawal.

He shrugged. He hadn't exhibited any finesse, or even his customary good manners. Instead he'd left her to wake alone. He'd been more brutal, perhaps, than strictly necessary. But he didn't want her harbouring illusions. He wasn't after a permanent relationship.

But an affair—mutually satisfying—now, that was something completely different.

He felt the unfamiliar stretch of facial muscles as his mouth curved into a smile.

Time and again today he'd found himself succumbing to temptation: reaching for his keys, calculating how long it would take to drive home, race up the stairs and find her. Perhaps she'd even be in bed, waiting for him, as eager for his touch as he was for hers.

But no. It was late afternoon. She'd have vacated his bed hours ago.

He'd deliberately kept away long enough to ensure there was no misunderstanding between them. He didn't want her expecting more from him than he was prepared to give.

His nights would be hers, as long as it suited them both. But by day he had other duties. He ignored the fact that he'd just cancelled his last meeting so he could hurry back to her. He was a man, after all, not a machine. And no sane man would opt for a late-afternoon meeting when he could have Sophie instead.

He ignored too the guilty suspicion that he'd made his point too blatantly. He could have called her earlier and explained he'd be away all day. He could have left her a message this morning. In fact, he could have woken her when he left their bed. Except he'd been scared that he might be tempted to remain there, heedless of all else.

Costas had never experienced a craving that could compare with his appetite for this one woman. He didn't know how to handle it.

Had he been a coward? Had he hurt her?

No. He'd been decisive, sensible. He'd started as he meant to go on. He knew Sophie, so open and honest, would appreciate that in the long run.

And after all, she'd waited for him on the beach last night. Clearly she now accepted his terms: no emotional ties, no plans for the future.

If she was disappointed this morning, well, he'd found it hard to leave her too. And he'd make it up to her.

Anticipation clenched his stomach muscles as he slowed for the electronic gates to open then nosed the car onto his private road.

Fleetingly this morning he'd felt guilt that he'd taken advantage of a guest under his roof. But he hadn't been able to sustain the remorse, not as the memories flooded back of the incredible night they'd shared.

It had been debatable who had seduced whom down on the shore. She was a natural siren, luring him to forget his scruples, his hesitation, everything but the need for her in his arms.

His breath snagged in his chest. He imagined her lying in sated abandonment in the centre of his bed. Waiting for his touch to bring her to passionate life again.

His foot slid forward on the accelerator as he pictured himself igniting her passion with his hands, his mouth, his body. He wanted her again. But then he'd wanted her all night and all day. Had been aroused time and again by the scent of her arousal, the magic of her flesh against his and the slumberous eroticism of her heavy-lidded eyes when she woke to his caresses.

Her absolute responsiveness had stunned him, urging him on to want, to take more than he ever had from a woman before. And she'd revelled in it, answering his desire with her own urgent need, provoking him to love her longer, harder, more completely than he'd thought possible.

He ached as hunger, unabated and white hot, took hold again.

He'd received excellent news today from Eleni's doctors. The best news. And he knew just how to celebrate it.

'Yes, *kyrie,* she went out some time ago, towards the sea, I think.' His housekeeper paused, frowning. 'She didn't look well. She was so pale, and she hasn't eaten anything, not even a morsel.'

Foreboding slammed into him, carving a hollow in his stomach. He'd *known* something was wrong. Had sensed it as soon as he'd failed to find Sophie in the house.

'Ah, here she is now,' said the housekeeper, tilting her head. Then he heard it, the sound of the front door and Sophie's light step across the foyer. 'Shall I—?'

'No. It's all right.' He was already turning away, ignoring the speculative gleam in his housekeeper's eyes.

He strode down the hallway, but Sophie had disappeared from the entrance hall. He took the stairs two at a time, an atavistic presentiment of trouble urging him to hurry.

He pushed open her door and there she was, wearing the clothes he'd chosen for her this morning. And somehow that fact was even more intimate than all last night's desperate loving.

Home. I've come home at last.

Something warm and tender, a stunning new sensation, curved tight in his chest as he looked at her. It held him spellbound for one long moment.

Then common sense reasserted itself and he breathed again.

Lust. That was what he felt. Simple. Uncomplicated. Easily assuaged.

Her hair fanned round her shoulders as she spun to face him.

He remembered the scent of those tresses, the impossibly soft texture of them sliding through his hands, teasing his flesh.

His automatic step towards her ended abruptly and he pulled up short, surveying her drawn face. His hand dropped to his side and a different sort of tension clamped his body into immobility.

Her face was a rigid mask. Her mouth clamped hard as if in pain. And her eyes—they were huge and shadowed.

'Sophie? What's wrong?' A piercing shard of fear sliced into him as he looked into her eyes. She was hurting, surely. He could barely believe it was the same woman he'd left warm, willing and satisfied in his bed.

'Nothing's wrong.' Her voice was light and high, but brittle as glass.

She opened her wardrobe door and bent to deposit a pair of sandals inside. When she turned round there was a wash of colour high on her cheekbones. It only accentuated the unusual pallor of her face.

What on earth was going on?

'Where have you been?' he demanded. Something must have happened in his absence.

'Just down to the beach.' She spun on her foot and headed for the bathroom, a bundle of clothes in her arms.

He'd taken just two paces when she came back, her hands empty this time.

'I was collecting my clothes from last night.'

Now the sweep of colour extended down her throat. She didn't meet his eyes but stood alone, staring blankly over his shoulder as if the sight of him pained her.

He frowned, trying to ignore the urgent clamour of his senses that urged him to march over and sweep her into his arms. He wanted to comfort her, for something was clearly, awfully wrong. Yet the way she held herself, as if a single touch might shatter her, held him back.

'You're back early,' she said at last and he heard the faintest echo of something—sarcasm—in her tone.

Ah, that was it. She objected to being left alone all day—was feeling neglected.

Costas brushed aside the voice of his conscience—the voice that agreed with her. That insisted he'd behaved appallingly.

This was no hard-edged business rival he faced, nor was it the immature, self-centred woman he'd made the mistake of marrying. This was Sophie: sweet, honest and caring.

But that didn't matter, he told himself again. He'd done the right thing. He didn't have time for emotional entanglements. He was simply being honest with her, making sure she didn't read too much into their intimacy.

Perhaps in his haste to get away, to put the situation in perspective and make sense of his intense reaction to her, he'd been brutal. But that could be remedied.

His pulse quickened at the prospect of soothing her ruffled ego.

'I had a lot to do,' he began.

'Of course.' She nodded. 'The hospital. And your business. You must have work to catch up on after all the time you've spent away from it.'

His brows pulled together in a frown as he tried to read her blank expression. An uncomfortable sensation clawed at him.

Guilt? After all, he'd manufactured those meetings this afternoon—seeking an excuse to keep away. He didn't do business personally in Heraklion any more. He worked from offices in Athens and New York, or here at home, where the latest telecommunications equipment allowed him to keep in touch with his worldwide enterprises.

He wasn't accustomed to using subterfuge. The feeling made him uncomfortable.

'You're not annoyed?'

He scrutinised her reaction, strangely piqued that she should accept his neglect so easily. Where was her fire? Where was the passionate, intense woman who'd captured his...interest... from the first?

'Why should I be annoyed?' She stared straight back at him and shrugged, wide-eyed and with palms spread towards him.

'You're a very important man with a commercial empire to run. And I...' She swallowed suddenly and blinked. 'I was tired. I slept for hours.'

Something wasn't right. Despite her direct look, despite her words, something was definitely amiss. He took a step towards her.

'But I must admit,' she said quickly, jutting her chin, 'where I come from it's customary at least to thank the woman you've spent the night with.' Her eyes blazed now, scorching him where he stood. 'To do it in person is best. But a note or at least a phone call would suffice. It's considered bad manners to lope off without a word.'

Her words rooted him to the spot. Not because of the searing temper he read behind them—that was almost welcome after her unnatural calm. But the implication of what she'd said—*where I come from...*

She was lecturing him on post-coital etiquette—with the insouciance of a woman who knew just what she was talking about.

A surge of white-hot jealousy rocked him. It was so intense and immediate that he clenched his fists against the need to find a violent outlet for his feelings.

How many men had shared her bed in Australia?

Did she care for any of them? Even one of them?

The thought of Sophie, *his* Sophie, with another man, *ever,* was untenable. He shook his head, trying to clear the red fog of rage that blinded him.

'That's not something you'll need to worry about again,' he growled, closing the distance between them with a single stride. 'There'll be no more men in your bed.'

'Are you including yourself in that?' Her brows arched haughtily as she tipped her head up to meet him head-on.

'Don't play games, Sophie. You know what I mean.' He gathered in a huge, sustaining breath. The depth of his jealousy, and its suddenness, made his head spin. He reacted instinctively. 'You're mine now. There won't be any other men in your life, much less anywhere near your bed!'

She glared back at him, her eyes flashing gold fire. Her nostrils flared and her hands fisted on her hips as she stood, toe to toe against him.

What a woman she was! Beautiful and strong and passionate. The sexiest woman he'd ever known.

His woman, intoned the possessive voice that had echoed in his ears all through the night.

'I don't think that's any of your business,' she said, her words slow and deliberate.

He scowled. What sort of nonsense was this? 'Of course it's my business. You and I—'

'What makes you think you have exclusive rights over me?' Her brow pleated in mock-concentration and her head tilted to one side as if to reinforce her point. 'I don't remember any discussion of that last night.'

'There was no discussion last night. We didn't—'

'Then perhaps I should make it clear to you now,' she said, just as if he hadn't spoken. 'I'm my own woman, Costas Palamidis. I don't belong to you. Or to any other man.' She stared past him, at a point somewhere over his shoulder. 'Last night doesn't entitle you to determine anything at all about the way I live my life.'

The blood pounded loud in Costas' ears, a deafening roar that almost obliterated the last of her declaration. Almost, but unfortunately not quite.

She was exerting her independence.

From him!

He gritted his teeth against the primitive howl of rage that welled in his throat.

This woman drove him crazy, awoke the most barbaric of impulses in him. He could fully understand the urge of less civilised men to keep their women cloistered at home. Preferably tied to the bed.

'Surely,' he said at last in an unsteady voice, 'you're not trying to convince me you're promiscuous.'

He caught the horrified expression in her eyes and repressed a satisfied smile. 'I'd find it hard to believe you're the sort of woman who keeps a couple of guys on a string.' Despite what he'd originally thought.

There, he'd called her bluff and it had worked, that was obvious from the sag of her shoulders and the way she bit her lip. He wanted to reach out and brush his fingers over that luscious bottom lip, ease the hurt with the caress of his own mouth. And then perhaps lead her a step or two back towards the mattress, so conveniently located just behind her.

'You're right,' she said, but her voice was tight. 'That's not what I meant.'

Her gaze slid from his. She took a slow breath and he watched her breasts rise with it. He wanted her naked. Now. His eyes flickered to the bed. He was already planning how he'd have her when her voice jerked him back to the present.

'You made it plain what you wanted from me. A single night, you said.' Her eyes met his again and something slammed hard into his solar plexus at the expression he saw there. 'You wanted sex. That's all. Sex and release.' Molten gold burned in her eyes, brighter with each word.

'Well, you've had your night and now it's over.'

'You must be joking. *Glikia mou!*' He spread his hands in a gesture of amazement. 'After last night you can't expect this to stop so easily. The way we were together…it was incredible.'

A perfunctory smile curved her lips for an instant then disappeared. 'I'm glad you thought so. But nevertheless it's over.'

Costas shook his head, dumbfounded as never before. Sophie was *rejecting* him? After all that had passed between them last night?

It was impossible. Unbelievable.

His eyes narrowed as he took in her wary stance, the rapid rise and fall of her breasts. She was hoaxing. That was it. She was trying to bargain for more. He'd wounded her pride with his clumsy behaviour this morning and now she wanted him to grovel.

He wouldn't grovel, but he'd apologise. After all, she deserved it. He'd behaved like a lout.

'*Sophie mou.*' He lifted his hand towards her and was stunned when she stepped away from him.

He frowned. There was no need to play hard to get. He was a reasonable man, after all.

'I apologise for leaving you the way I did this morning. I should have woken you, or rung earlier in the day. I—'

She shook her head. 'There's no need to apologise,' she interrupted, though the over-bright glitter of her eyes belied her words. 'Last night was wonderful, but now it's finished. As you said, we both needed the release. And now we can go our separate ways with no regrets.'

Slowly the words penetrated his stunned brain. And then *déjà vu* cannoned into him, like a blow to the gut.

The expression on her face, the challenging stance and jutting chin. Just so had Fotini looked when he'd confronted her with his concerns about her safety. About her late-night celebrations with dubious new friends, about his suspicions that her herbal 'pick-me-up' tablets were something far more dangerous. She'd been defiant, amused, uncaring.

He swiped a hand over his face, trying to dislodge the memories and the devastating seed of doubt they planted in his mind. Two girls from the same family. Two women from the house of Liakos.

Was the independent spirit he'd so admired in Sophie a blind for something less palatable?

No! He didn't believe it. This was Sophie, sweet and caring. Not Fotini.

'It's over,' she reiterated. 'And now it's time to move on.' And with the words she turned away from him, as if to leave.

His hand shot out and circled her upper arm before she'd even taken a step. Her smooth flesh was warm beneath his fingers, soft as silk. But not as soft as her belly, or the indescribably tender skin of her inner thighs.

'No!' He stopped, trying to get control over his voice. 'It's not over, Sophie.'

She lifted her face and for an instant her expression was vivid, bright, like the sun in summer. And then a shutter came down, hiding her thoughts.

Costas groped for words, tried to get his brain into gear. But all he could think of was that she'd done the impossible—had rejected him, decided she wanted no more from him than a one-night stand.

The seductive, feminine scent of her skin made his nostrils flare and his blood quicken. It only fed his confusion and anger.

'What if you're pregnant?' he bit out.

He saw the flicker of shock in her face. Felt her stiffen beneath his hands. For an instant her eyes blazed with golden light, and then she turned her head away.

'And that would change things?' Her voice had an oddly muffled quality.

'*Sto Diavolo!* It would change everything. A child…' He paused, dragging in a deep breath. He'd said the first thing that had surged into his numbed brain. But now the idea had lodged there.

How could he want another child when he had Eleni? How could he face the possibility of such trauma again? But despite the fear, he recognised excitement tremble to life in the pit of his stomach.

A child. His and Sophie's. An invisible hand squeezed his heart. What a gift that would be.

'You know I take my family responsibilities seriously.' Somehow he managed to keep his voice even as he looked down at her.

'Then it's just as well that's not a possibility.'

'Of course it's a possibility,' he thundered. 'We had unprotected sex, not once, but several times last night.'

That was what had been at the back of his mind down on the beach, the vague notion of something not right. But it hadn't stopped him. Lord help him, even if he'd realised at the time, he doubted he'd have been able to pull back from her. His need for Sophie had been elemental, unstoppable.

He looked down into her staring eyes. Had she been too caught up in their mutual passion to realise he hadn't used a condom? Inevitably the idea pleased him, softening his temper into something else. His iron hard grip on her arm loosened and he slid his fingers down her tender flesh, stroking. She trembled under his touch as she always did.

Abruptly she tore herself away and paced over to the windows, presenting him with her hunched shoulders. Something—pain—twisted deep inside him at her rebuff.

'There's absolutely no chance I'm pregnant,' she said in a cold, precise voice that speared him like a knife.

Bright sunlight blurred her outline, and for an instant it was another girl who stood there. Another bloodless voice that echoed between them, taunting him.

Memories again. Stronger this time.

He'd married Fotini because he'd decided he needed a wife. But the marriage had held none of the peace, the trust or even companionship that he'd expected would grow with time.

And now he'd ignored his better judgement, shoved aside every caution and succumbed to the temptation of this woman, Fotini's cousin. She was like fire in his blood, destroying his logic and his self-control.

Two girls so different.

But could there be similarities as well?

Nausea churned in his stomach at the possibility.

'What if you're mistaken, Sophie?' He forced the words out, sickened by the fact that he even had to ask. 'What if you *are* pregnant? Would you expect me to pay for the abortion?'

CHAPTER FIFTEEN

SOPHIE HAD THOUGHT an hour ago that she could bear the truth. Just. But this was torture. Listening to the man she loved. Yes— the man she *loved,* lashing her heart with his blatant contempt.

What more did he want from her?

He'd taken her body. He'd taken her trust, her love, her tentative hopes and dreams and trampled them underfoot.

Oh, it hadn't been his fault. He'd warned her, had been totally honest. He'd told her in no uncertain terms that his need for her was at the most basic, physical level only. He'd left her under no illusion that he wanted a relationship with her.

It had been her own naïve fault that she'd succumbed to him with such self-destructive passion. Hurting as she was, needing comfort and overwhelmed by feelings she'd never before experienced, she'd turned to him.

And then, when it was too late, she'd assumed that the situation had changed, that he felt it now too—the bond between them.

How could he *not* feel something so powerful?

She'd given herself joyfully, loved him with her heart and soul, not just her body.

And today she'd woken to the harsh truth. She'd deluded herself. He simply didn't love her.

So she'd gathered the tatters of her self-respect about her and decided not to let him see how much she was hurting. Her plan was to escape, soon, with her dignity intact if possible. She'd remove herself far from his vicinity in the hope that time might heal her battered heart.

She'd been coping, just, with the trauma of seeing him again. It had been virtually impossible but she'd hidden her emotions as best she could.

But now he'd turned into a vengeful stranger and she didn't think she could keep up the pretence of indifference much longer.

'Answer me, Sophie! Would you come to me to fund an abortion?'

'That question doesn't deserve an answer.' Stubbornly she stared out the window, eyes blinking at the bright blue cloudless sky. The serene, blazing Greek sun half-blinded her—mocking her pretensions in ever hoping for a future with this man.

A large hand grabbed her elbow and Costas swung her around so abruptly she almost fell. But he was so close, his other hand already supporting her, that she merely stumbled. The inevitable tremor spread from his touch along her arms, reminding her of those hours not long ago when his caress had been searingly tender, heartbreakingly gentle.

And she hated her weakness in remembering.

His eyes fired with unholy anger as he thrust his belligerent face towards hers. Every plane, every angle was harsh and unforgiving.

'Answer me!'

Fear scudded through her, now she was up close to such potent rage. She could feel his fury in his hands, clamped so hard on her arms that she had pins and needles from the restricted blood flow. She could smell it in his blood-hot masculine scent, taste it in the heat of his breath on her face.

But she refused to be cowed. His anger fuelled her courage. How dare he talk to her like that?

'And which part of that scenario would bother you most, *Kyrie Palamidis?* The abortion itself or me asking you to foot the bill?'

'*Christos!*' He shook her once, twice, as a flurry of fierce Greek split the air.

Sophie's head swam as she stared up into his dark face. She

didn't recognise the man she saw. He looked as savage, as dangerous as a predator, moving in for the kill.

'You will not dispose of any child of mine as if it were some inconvenience,' he snarled.

'And you will stop making insulting assumptions about me,' she gasped between strangled breaths. Fruitlessly she tried to wrest herself from his punishing hold. Now, before the emotion clogging her throat welled into shameful tears.

She'd done nothing wrong. She didn't deserve his contempt!

'I am *not* pregnant with your precious baby,' she spat at him. 'And even if I were, I wouldn't consider a termination.' She stopped to drag down air into a chest so tight she couldn't seem to fill it with oxygen. 'More than that, you're the last person I'd ever accept money from.'

Her hair swirled round her face as she struggled to break his grip. She was so frantic to escape she didn't notice the way he shifted his weight, crowding closer.

'Enough! You will hurt yourself if you don't calm down.'

Inexorably he drew her arms back so he could shackle both her wrists in his hands. She was no match for his strength. She couldn't prevent him from bowing her back over his other arm.

She was helpless against his power. And against the savage determination she read in his eyes.

'Let me go—' Her protest ended in muffled outrage as his mouth blocked hers.

Savagely he kissed her, like some rapacious thief, plundering so thoroughly that she could barely breathe. He bruised her lips, invaded her mouth with a blatant, masculine possessiveness that stamped his domination on her.

Shock held her in its grasp and she almost choked on a sob. There was no tenderness here. No shred of the magic that had enthralled her last night. This time the hard length of his body was a weapon, crushing her into absolute submission.

After her hopes and tender dreams last night, she felt defiled. The pain of her disillusionment was so raw she thought her heart would bleed.

'Sophie.' The unrelenting pressure abated a fraction and his words feathered across her swollen lips. 'You make me wild. I can't believe…'

Hot kisses trawled down her chin, her neck, to her collar-bone. He pressed his mouth to the tender flesh there, sucking gently till she shuddered in unwilling response. He knew every erogenous zone on her body—he'd spent the night learning each one.

To Sophie's horror she felt the familiar electric charge of excitement skitter through her. She was trembling, but not solely with outrage.

He took her mouth again, but gently, so tenderly that she might have been some fragile, breakable treasure. He slid his lips along hers as if seeking permission to enter. His tongue flicked out, drawing her opposition from her.

His hand came up to hold her breast, squeeze it, sending another heated, frantic response through her nerve-endings. Dimly she registered the hollow feeling between her legs. The wanting. His caress slowed as he circled her nipple, just as his tongue stroked her mouth.

She moaned and felt the caress of his arm at her back, cradling her against him.

Suddenly desire was a swirling, dazzling force within her, loosening every taut muscle, leaving her body defenceless, willing, even when she *knew* she had to resist. Feebly she fought the onslaught against her senses.

'Glikia mou,' he whispered, his voice so deep she felt the words as much as heard them. 'You make me mindless, Sophie.' His fingers tightened on her breast and sensation juddered through her. 'I want you. Now.'

If he hadn't spoken he might even have got what he wanted. She was aroused, eager, panting for him.

After all he'd said and done!

The realisation shamed her with the knowledge of her appalling weakness. But his words penetrated her numbed brain even as her body responded ecstatically to his caresses. That was when she discovered he'd released her wrists.

Adrenaline surged through her, stiffening her resolve and her body. She shoved with all her might, bringing her knee up sharply in a vicious thrust that should have crippled him.

But his assault on her senses had weakened her. Either that or he could read her mind. He side-stepped just as her knee slammed up. She was off balance and would have fallen if it weren't for his hands pulling her upright.

'Don't touch me!' She shrugged out of his hold and stumbled back a few paces. 'Don't come near me,' she gasped, chest heaving for breath. Her heart hammered like a set of pistons.

'Sophie.' He paced towards her and she flinched.

'Stay away!'

'You don't mean that.' His voice was a low, persuasive murmur. It made her skin prickle, eager for the delights he could bestow.

'I mean what I say. I don't need some arrogant male to tell me what I want.'

'Sophie, I know you're upset. But it doesn't have to be like this. You know how good it is between us.'

She shook her head. He saw her as a convenient lay. Better than a sleeping tablet to get him through the long nights.

'I don't want you to touch me. Ever.'

He crossed his arms. His legs were already planted wide apart and he looked impossibly big and powerful. What hope did she have if he refused to listen? She didn't trust her treacherous body not to respond if he tried to seduce her again.

There was a knowing glint in his eyes and his mouth twisted up at one side. 'I know how much you want me, Sophie. How you burn for me.'

He stalked closer as he spoke, the words rolling off his seductive tongue in a murmur that made her body tighten. 'I've never had such an eager lover.'

She gritted her teeth. 'How do I get through to you? One night was enough and now it's over.' She stared hard into his glittering eyes and deliberately played her last card. 'Unless you intend to use force.'

'What are you talking about?' His brows dipped into a ferocious scowl. 'You must know I would never use force on a woman.' He drew himself up to his full looming height and looked down his nose at her. As if she'd dared to insult him!

'Then what do you call this?' She thrust her arms out in front of her, silent witness to the power he'd unleashed to hold her still. Red marks encircled each wrist. There was no pain. Not now. But there'd be bruises soon.

His face froze and his golden skin paled. She watched his convulsive swallow as he realised what he'd done.

'I must apologise,' he said in a stifled voice. 'It is no excuse to say that I didn't realise how tightly I held you. But be assured you have nothing to fear. It will never happen again.'

She let her arms drop to her sides, curiously drained. 'Let it end,' she pleaded, feeling the weight of emotional exhaustion descend onto her shoulders. 'It was…nice, while it lasted. But I don't need a relationship any more than you do. Not now. It would be too messy.'

She turned away, hoping he wouldn't call her bluff. Not now her eyes had filled with useless tears.

'We've both been through a rough time and last night—just happened,' she said, whispering to conceal the wobble in her voice. 'But now I need to get on with my own life.' She wrapped her arms round herself, squeezing as if she could force back the pain welling up inside her.

If she could just hold on until he left her alone.

'You're right, of course.' His words were clipped, precise, his voice a stranger's. 'Since neither of us is in a position to want more than physical release from a partner, it's best if we put last night behind us.'

Each word bit into her, carving away the last of her defences. She'd been right. Absolutely right. How foolish of her to cling to that final, stubborn hope that Costas would object. That he'd swear it was more than lust between them. That he felt tenderness for her, even love.

She squeezed shut her eyes and bit her lip, praying for the strength to see out this scene without giving herself away.

She had nothing left. Nothing at all but the remnants of her pride.

The silence was so loud it pulsed between them. But she didn't dare turn round. She knew her anguish would be obvious in her face.

And then she heard it—the sound she'd been praying for. And dreading. The sound of his measured pace crossing the room. The quiet, definite click of the door behind him.

Costas Palamidis had done what she asked and walked out of her life.

CHAPTER SIXTEEN

LEAVING THE NEXT DAY was harder than Sophie had expected.

Not that she'd had to confront Costas again. By mutual consent they'd avoided each other yesterday evening. The house was big enough to accommodate them both in perfect isolation. And she hadn't sought him out today after she'd packed her suitcase and organised a lift into town.

She'd wondered if he might try to prevent her leaving, persuade her to stay. Her pulse had raced at the possibility, wondering if she'd have the strength to resist his persuasion if he exerted himself. But he'd already taken an early-morning flight to Athens to deal in person with some urgent business. His house-keeper had been flustered, concerned at her departure while the *kyrios* was away.

But to Sophie it was a tremendous relief. She could pretend she was glad not to have to face him again. That it would be easier this way. No embarrassing farewells, no regrets.

A pity she didn't really believe that.

Instead, as the villa disappeared behind her, she felt stretched too thin, as if she'd left some part of herself behind. The part she'd left with Costas.

And then she had to face the hospital farewells. Her grandfather already knew she was only in Crete for a short time. He said nothing when she explained about the flight today. But she'd seen the disappointment in his eyes. Which only made her feel worse.

ANNIE WEST

Despite his treatment of her mother, and his antiquated views, he was family. She couldn't turn her back on him completely. Her eyes prickled as she squeezed his hand and promised to visit again when she'd tidied up her mother's affairs.

She'd be back. But under her own steam this time. And she'd make a point of steering well clear of Costas Palamidis. Might even take her grandfather up on his gruff offer to stay with him when he was released from hospital.

The farewell to Eleni was no easier. Sophie hadn't realised how close they'd become until she had to say goodbye. And the little girl's stoic smile, just a little wobbly, was almost Sophie's undoing.

But what could she do? It was impossible to stay in Costas' home any longer. And the thought of seeing him every day, as she would if she continued to visit Eleni, was untenable.

She'd planned to leave soon anyway. She couldn't put her life on hold forever, even for such a little sweetie as Eleni. The parting had always been inevitable. But that didn't make it any easier.

She wondered if she'd be able to see Eleni again when she returned to Greece, and yet avoid Costas.

Hell! What a mess this was.

Yet she had no doubts about what she was doing. For her own sanity she had to leave. Now. She couldn't afford to torture herself, being so close to the man she loved and couldn't have.

She'd done the right thing, pushing him away. Of course she had. She wasn't cut out for an affair. She wanted a future. The chance of lasting happiness with someone who cared for her as much as she loved him.

Another night in the Palamidis mansion might just destroy the final tatters of her self-respect. Even now she couldn't risk the temptation to be alone with Costas. She was so weak-willed when it came to him.

'*Thespinis?* Are you all right?'

Sophie blinked back hot tears at the sound of Yiorgos' words and fumbled in her bag for sunglasses.

'I'm OK, thanks. The sun is so bright, isn't it?' She turned her head and watched the outskirts of Heraklion slide by. Soon now she'd be at the airport. But she wouldn't relax till she was off the island. She had enough money to get to Athens. Then she'd visit the embassy. Find out how she could finance the flight to Sydney. Surely they'd lend her the money? And she could pay it back when she got home.

Home.

That empty house didn't feel like home any more. The sooner she sold it and found a little flat the better. She could organise another trip to see her grandfather and then look around for permanent work. Speech pathologists were always in demand.

The car slid to a halt at the airport entrance. By the time she fumbled her way free of the seat belt, Yiorgos had collected her bag and held the door open for her.

'Are you sure, *thespinis,* that you're all right?' His handsome features puckered in a concerned frown.

'I'm fine. Thanks.' She dredged up a smile and held out her hand for her bag.

'No, no!' He was horrified. He clasped the suitcase close then gestured for her to precede him. It was unthinkable, apparently, for her to be left alone to enter the airport.

Yiorgos remained with her through the flight check-in and would have stayed longer, she was sure, except for a peremptory summons on his cellphone. The way he snapped to attention convinced her it was Costas on the line. Her heart lurched, realising this was the closest she'd ever come again to the man she loved.

She pushed back her shoulders and walked away to find a seat while she waited to board the plane.

The wait went on and on. Too nervous to sit for long, she paced continually, but the time crawled by. Eventually she looked at her watch and realised the flight should have been called. Had she missed it?

No. It was there on the board. Delayed.

Sophie bit back a frustrated oath.

So there was a slight delay. It didn't matter. It wasn't as if she had a connecting flight booked. All she had to do was get into

Athens and find a cheap *pension* for the night. Then tomorrow she'd visit the embassy and everything would be settled.

'Miss Paterson?' There was a discreet cough behind her and she swung round. Two men stood there. One in uniform and the other in a grey suit that strained over his rotund form.

'Yes? I'm Sophie Paterson.'

'Excellent,' said the man in the suit. She saw a flash of gold as he smiled. 'Would you mind coming with us, please?'

'What's wrong? My flight is due—'

'Nothing is wrong,' he assured her, gesturing for her to accompany them. 'The flight is delayed but not for much longer. In the meantime,' he led her across the waiting area towards an unmarked door, 'there is a message for you.'

'For me?' She swung round. Who could have left a message for her? She gazed at the plump little man beside her but got only an unctuous smile. And the uniformed guy behind him looked so serious she felt a thrill of fear skitter up her spine.

'Are you sure there's not a problem?'

'No, no.' The man beside her opened the door and gestured for her to precede him. 'As I said, just a message.'

He ushered her into what was clearly an interview room. Furnished only with a table and a couple of chairs. Automatically Sophie wondered what was wrong.

She swung round just as the door closed behind her. The guard hadn't come in. She assumed he was stationed outside the room. The idea made the hair prickle on the back of her neck.

'If there's a difficulty with my papers—'

'No, no. Nothing like that.' Again the stranger smiled, spreading his arms wide. 'Please, take a seat.'

'I'd rather stand, thank you.'

He tilted his head to one side. 'As you wish. I will just be a moment.' And with that he let himself out of another door. One she assumed led into the airport offices.

The room must be soundproofed. She couldn't hear anything. Not the people waiting for their flights nor the hum of engines. The realisation chilled her. She didn't know why she was here.

Or for how long. What if she missed her flight? It was the only one to Athens this afternoon. She didn't want to stay on Crete another night.

Sophie bit down on her lower lip. Panicking wouldn't help her. Whatever the problem she'd sort it out. She hadn't done anything wrong, after all.

The door opened and she swung round.

Her heart leapt into her throat and she would have stumbled if she hadn't grabbed on to the back of a chair.

Costas stood framed in the doorway.

'Sophie.' He paced towards her and the walls of the small room seemed to close in around her. His face was unreadable but the tense set of his shoulders was eloquent.

'What are you doing here?' Her voice sounded rusty.

'I need you.'

His dark velvet eyes held hers and the world tilted. He needed her?

'No.' She shook her head, holding the chair in a death grip.

But his gaze was so intense she felt as if he delved into the very heart of her, reading the secret she tried so desperately to hide. Her knees trembled as she looked up into his stark face.

'Yes.' Something pulsed between them. Raw and desperate. 'We need you Sophie.'

'We?'

'Eleni—'

'She's worse?' Sophie swallowed down the hard knot of anxiety that blocked her throat. It had only been a few hours since she'd left the hospital. Eleni had been fine then, though upset about Sophie's departure. Had she taken a turn for the worse?

Costas' face was grim as he held out his hand. 'She needs you. Now. You wouldn't deny her, would you?'

'But I can't. I have a flight.' She gestured helplessly to the other door.

Costas' hand sliced through the air between them. 'That means nothing. I can book you onto another flight when this is over. If you want.'

She stared up at him, noting the drawn look around his mouth, the stiff set to his jaw. Whatever had happened was life-and-death serious. Her anxiety notched up another level. Poor, brave little Eleni.

'You promise?'

'When you want a flight I will personally see you on board.'

She believed him. Whatever else he might be, Costas was a man of his word. He'd been straight down the line with her. No prevaricating, no dressing up the truth with convenient euphemisms. He said what he meant.

'But why me—?'

'It's you she needs.'

Sophie frowned. Eleni had grown attached to her—it had been mutual, after all. But surely Eleni's father, her grandparents, were the ones who should be with her now?

'It's time we left.' He stepped close, stretching out his hand as if to take her arm. She felt the fierce heat of his body reaching out to her, but then his hand dropped to his side. He maintained a small but telling distance.

And she was grateful for it. Even this close the tension seemed to shimmer between them, the air charged with a force that she couldn't hope to ignore.

'I'll have to make arrangements for my luggage.'

'It's been taken care of.' He motioned for her to lead the way out of the room. 'It's all in hand.'

'In hand?' In the act of walking out the door she stopped and spun round to stare at him. 'You did that without even asking me?'

'Sophie.' She'd never heard this dreadful urgency in his voice before. 'It was necessary. Believe me. This is an emergency.'

His face was set hard. But something about his eyes told her this really *mattered*. More even than her heartbreak. Or her pride. Pain radiated from him. And more than that—uncertainty. That was so remarkable it convinced her as nothing else could.

Eleni's condition must be serious.

His pain tore at her already lacerated heart. She shook her

head, wondering helplessly how she could feel so much for a man who didn't want her. How had *his* pain become hers?

But so it was. Despite everything—her anger and her hurt— she didn't want him to suffer. Not with the raw agony she saw staring back at her from his proud features.

His arm wrapped round her shoulders and he propelled her towards the door. His hold was light, but she sensed the steel behind it.

Her body reacted predictably. A tremor started somewhere deep inside her, spreading out until she was weak with barely suppressed longing.

The short man in the grey suit was in the corridor, waiting for them. 'Everything is all right, *Kyrie Palamidis?*'

'Yes.' Costas reached out and shook his hand, but kept his left arm around her. 'Thank you for your assistance. I regret the inconvenience.'

'But that is nothing. Nothing at all. It was a pleasure to assist in such circumstances.'

'And it was greatly appreciated.'

The other man beamed.

'Now we must leave.' Costas was already ushering Sophie down the hall.

'What inconvenience?' she asked as they emerged near the airport entrance.

The muscles in his arm bunched around her as they walked rapidly towards the exit. 'Holding up your flight.'

'What?'

'It was easier to have you and your luggage taken off the plane before it departed than having it turn around.'

She stumbled to a halt and stared up into his face. He wasn't joking. 'You'd do that?'

He shrugged and somehow the action pulled her closer to him, close enough to recognise the hard, tantalising strength of his superb body. For his natural scent to tease her nostrils and ignite a flare of forbidden desire in her feminine core.

'Of course. If it was necessary.' The commanding tilt of his head, the arrogant line of his nose and the decisive glint in his eyes told her he wasn't joking. This was a man to whom power was a natural extension of his will. He wouldn't baulk at using it when it suited his needs.

She'd known he was influential. But would he really be able to have a jet turn around in mid-flight?

'*Ela*. Come, Sophie. This is not the place.'

Of course not. Eleni needed them.

'OK. Let's go to the hospital.' She stepped forward, shrugging to remove his hold. For a moment she thought he wouldn't let her go. His arm clenched tighter round her. Then, to her immense relief, it dropped away. She breathed easier, glad of even this minimal space between them.

Yiorgos was waiting beside the limousine, his face anxious. He broke into a strained smile as they both appeared.

'The luggage?' Costas prompted as he ushered her into the spacious back section of the vehicle.

'Already in the boot, *kyrie*.'

And within seconds they pulled away, leaving the airport behind. The privacy screen slid up, blocking them off from Yiorgos, emphasising the empty silence in the vehicle. Sophie slid to one corner of the wide back seat, well away from the daunting presence of the man beside her.

Her emotions were a confused jumble. Fear for Sophie. Numb horror that she had to face Costas again after what had passed between them. And, could it be? Yes, relief that she wasn't leaving Crete just yet.

From the moment Costas had appeared in that bare little room and demanded she accompany him, it had been so unreal. For one cruelly short moment she'd really thought he'd come because he needed her himself. Because he couldn't bear to let her go. The idea had brought a fizz of searing excitement to her bloodstream.

But she'd known, as soon as he mentioned Eleni, that it was his daughter who needed her. That was why he'd brought her to Greece after all. Her disappointment had been so acute that for an instant she'd even thought of refusing to go with him. But she could never turn her back on Eleni. She loved the little girl. Almost as deeply as she loved Eleni's father.

Sophie's heart sank at the idea of an emergency severe enough to recall her from a flight to Athens.

She turned her head towards the window, blindly staring out at the passing scene.

Costas sat back in the opposite corner, watching Sophie. His heart still pounded from the adrenaline in his bloodstream. He'd barely been in time to prevent her departure. It had been so close it scared him.

Now she was here, secure in his car. He waited for the sense of satisfaction to come. After all, he'd got what he wanted. Almost. She'd followed him like a lamb once he mentioned Eleni.

But he felt no lessening of the tension that gripped him in its vice. There were no self-satisfied congratulations.

For Sophie looked miserable, hunched like a prisoner in the corner. Exhaustion etched shadows in the contours of her face and her shoulders slumped heavily. His gaze dropped to her hands, clasped tight in her lap, and he shuddered.

On one arm she wore a wide, beaded bangle. But her other arm was bare and his stomach lurched at the sight of the bruise ringing her delicate wrist. Nausea welled in him.

He'd done that. He'd hurt her—used his physical superiority to try controlling her.

Costas drew a ragged breath, stunned at the evidence of his barbaric behaviour. In all his life he'd *never* used force on a woman. The very idea was anathema. Even in those darkest days, when Fotini had driven him to despair and lashing fury, he had never come close to touching her in violence.

How could Sophie ever trust him after such a disgraceful act? No man of honour would do such a thing.

But then his honour was a tainted thing, wasn't it? He'd taken advantage of her in the worst possible way. She'd been so vulnerable. So deserving of his protection. A guest. The donor who was saving his daughter's life. A member of Eleni's family. A woman grieving her own terrible loss and far from home.

Any one of those considerations should have ensured he treated her with absolute courtesy and care.

But none of it had mattered enough to stop him.

Guilt slashed him. He'd been no protector. He'd been insane, consumed by his own rapacious need and his determination to have her on *his* terms.

He'd been ruthless, so desperate in his craving for her that he'd thrown away his honour to possess her. He'd subjected her to the risk of pregnancy without a second thought. In fact, some deep-buried part of him exalted in the possibility that she might be pregnant to him.

No wonder she hadn't waited to say farewell in person but had taken the opportunity to sneak away while he was absent. He should never have—

'What's going on?' Sophie swung round from her contemplation of the scenery to fix him with accusing eyes. 'This isn't the way to the hospital.'

Even in her confusion, with a frown marring her features, her beauty made his throat constrict.

'No, it's not,' he said, relieved that it was time to sort this out, once and for all. 'I'm taking you home.'

CHAPTER SEVENTEEN

HOME? THE WORD echoed in her ears. Home was an empty bungalow on the other side of the world.

And this was the coastal road leading to the Palamidis villa. The place where she'd known such hopes and such appalling disappointment.

Sophie stared into Costas' eyes. They were almost black—a sign, she'd learned, of strong emotion. And the way he looked at her—hungrily, so intensely that she should be frightened.

Her breath caught. Sensation shivered down her spine.

Just so had he gazed at her two nights ago when he'd loved her so wondrously.

'What's going on?' Suspicion flared as she took in his utter stillness. He was tensed, completely focused on her, like a predator watching its prey.

'You're not taking me to the hospital, are you?' Realisation came in a rush. But even so she couldn't quite believe what her brain was telling her.

'Not yet.'

'How is Eleni's condition?'

He hesitated infinitesimally. 'Physically she's doing remarkably well. She'll be coming home to us soon. But she was terribly upset about your plans to leave.'

'You lied to me.' The accusation was a whisper. Even in the face of the evidence Sophie couldn't imagine Costas telling an untruth. 'You deliberately made me believe Eleni's condition was worse.'

'All I said was—'

'I know what you said, damn you,' she gasped. 'How could you be so cruel? You made me think…'

Suddenly he seemed much closer, his wide shoulders and his dark, compelling face filling her vision. He reached for her hand, his fingers hard and warm, but she wrenched out of his grasp.

'I told you that we needed you.'

'And you lied.'

'No, I spoke the truth. We need you. Both of us.'

She shook her head, denying the flicker of hope in the chilled recesses of her heart. She was tired, so tired she couldn't cope with this right now. But one thing she knew without doubt: Costas Palamidis did not need her.

'Don't lie to me. I won't play your games.'

'It is no game, Sophie. Only once have I told you an untruth.' His gaze held hers and she couldn't look away. 'When I said I wanted you for a single night only. Do you remember?'

Oh, she remembered all right. Heat scorched her cheeks at the memory.

'It wasn't true, Sophie. I want more. So much more.'

Now it began to make some sort of crazy sense. Costas wanted more. And what Costas wanted Costas got. He'd decided one night wasn't enough. She supposed she should feel complimented that he found her so attractive.

But she didn't. She felt…sullied. It was her body he wanted. Not *her*.

He leaned close, his scent and his heat and his aura of energy encompassing her. But she had no difficulty pushing him away. Hard.

'Stay away from me,' she panted. 'I don't want you near me.'

'Sophie.' He reached out a hand and she slapped it back. The contact made her palm sting.

'Stay away!' Her voice rose. 'If you think I want anything more to do with you, you're wrong.'

Despite its luxurious size the limousine felt claustrophobically small. There wasn't enough air for them both in the charged atmosphere. And though he didn't touch her, Costas' very presence crowded her. His energy was a palpable force.

Suddenly he reached away from her, to a control panel on his side of the car. The screen between them and the driver slid down and Costas shot out some orders in rapid-fire Greek. Then the screen slid into place again and Costas turned back to her.

The car slowed and turned. But instead of swinging round in the direction they'd come from, it slid to a halt off the road. Dazed, Sophie stared out the window. She recognised this place, a little glade on the edge of an ancient olive grove. They'd left the main road and were already on Costas' estate. She hadn't even noticed them slow to pass the security system on their way in.

She heard Yiorgos get out and automatically reached for the door. She didn't know why they'd stopped here rather than at the house, but the sooner she got out into the fresh air, where she could put some distance between herself and Costas, the better.

Even as her fingers closed round the handle there came the soft, decisive click of the door locks engaging.

She swung round. Costas had his hand on the control panel.

'Unlock the door.'

'Soon. When we've talked.'

'We have nothing to discuss. It's all been said. We both know where we stand. And now I'd like to leave.' Her heart pounded against her ribs and her breathing shallowed as she fought to maintain an appearance of calm.

'There is still much to discuss, Sophie, before we both know where we stand.' His voice was deep and smooth but she heard the strain in it. 'You will be free to leave once we've discussed what's between us.'

She shook her head. 'You can't do that. You can't hold me against my will!'

'Only until you hear me out.' He reached for her hand and held it between both of his. She didn't bother to struggle—she knew his strength would win out. So she concentrated instead on pretending to ignore the barrage of sensations flooding her at his touch. The heat, the sizzle of delight, the ravenous need.

How could she respond so mindlessly? And to such a casual caress? She tilted her chin high. 'Then I hope you're prepared to face trial for abduction.'

He ignored the threat.

Horrified, she watched him raise her hand to his mouth, felt the caress of his lips against her flesh and almost closed her eyes at the memories evoked by the sensation. How her body still craved him.

'I mean it! I'll lay charges. And then what about your reputation? Think of the talk, all the rumours. The stain on your good name.'

'You must do as you think appropriate, *after* we've talked,' he murmured against her wrist and turned her hand over to kiss her palm.

Darts of fierce desire shot along her arm, arrowing straight to the hollow, aching core of her need. Her taut muscles loosened as his tongue lapped, rough velvet against her sensitive skin.

She struggled to focus. 'I don't want you. Don't you understand that? Where is your pride?' Surely that, if anything, would get through to him.

He looked up, his head still bent over her hand. His eyes were so hot she felt their incendiary heat burn deep inside as he met her gaze.

'*Agapi mou,* you need me as much as I need you. I was a fool yesterday to think I could ever walk away from you.'

He leaned closer, looming over her, and she fought the absurd impulse to bury her head on his shoulder and wrap her arms tight round him.

'Yiorgos will see us.' She was desperate for anything that would stop his inexorable assault on her senses. On her self-control.

'Yiorgos is already walking to the house.' His breath was hot on her face as he leaned closer still. 'We're on my private property. No one will disturb us. And anyway, the tinted windows give us privacy.'

Privacy for what? Her mind raced as she read the raw desire in his stark features.

'No!' Frantically she shoved against the rock-hard wall of his chest. But it was like pushing against unforgiving granite. 'I don't want—'

His mouth on her lips stopped her voice. His tongue stroked against hers, inviting the response that shivered just a breath away. He leaned into her, pressing her back into the soft corner of the padded seat, his hands roving, skimming her body as if frantic to rediscover her.

He didn't use force. If he had she would have been able to fight him.

But the devious brute used gentle, erotic persuasion. And that weapon, in this man's hands, was unstoppable. Sophie didn't have a hope.

She tasted him in her mouth, inhaled the tangy scent of him, felt the shiver of delight wherever his hands caressed. The fiery heat of his body was like a magnet, drawing her closer, inciting a passion so strong it overruled every last remnant of her will-power.

Their night of intimacy had merely set the seal on the emotion that had been growing inside her over the past weeks.

This was the man she loved. The man who'd stolen her heart. So bold, so strong. Handsome, tender, protective. The most sensitive, daring, passionate lover a woman could wish for. Her weak body, even her mind, worked against the memory of the devastating pain he'd inflicted on her.

No matter how far she ran. Even if she escaped back to Sydney, she'd never be free of her feelings for him.

He only had to take her in his arms, seduce her with the incredible tenderness he wielded so easily, and all her defences shattered.

She sighed into his open mouth as his hand brushed her breast, teasing, tempting, till she pressed forward and felt his palm close round her.

Her hands locked round the back of his neck and she didn't protest as he pushed her down against the seat. She sensed the urgency in him as his breathing changed, the rhythm of his heart hammering against hers quickened. His hands grew heavier, more urgent as they stroked her, lingering on the buttons of her shirt.

Sophie knew what he wanted. Here, in a parked car in broad daylight. And, lord help her, she wanted it too. Just one last time.

She'd regret it later. But she had no more lies left inside her. She couldn't pretend any longer.

He'd won.

She turned her head and nuzzled the hollow of his neck, breathing deep of the masculine scent of his arousal. His skin was steamy with the energy of sexual excitement.

'Sophie?' He lifted a hand to her cheek, his thumb brushing the skin below her eye.

'Ah, *Sophie mou*. Don't cry. Please don't cry.' His voice was a hoarse groan of pain.

She blinked and registered the scalding tears spilling down her cheeks. Tears for her discarded hopes.

There was a surge of movement. Strong hands, an even stronger body against hers. And then she was sitting up. But not on the luxurious limousine seat. Instead she was cradled on Costas' thighs, sitting sideways across him, pulled in close against his massive chest, her head resting on his shoulder and his arms wrapped tight around her.

He was trembling, his whole body tense and shivering beneath hers.

'I hurt you.' His words were a whisper against her hair. 'I'm sorry, Sophie. I've been a monster. I don't ever want to cause you pain again.'

She felt a hard sob well inside her at the sincerity in his husky voice. He might not want to hurt her but he couldn't help it. It was inevitable when she craved so much more from him than he could give.

Wordlessly she shook her head and leaned closer to him. Ridiculous to find comfort in the embrace of the man who was at the core of her unhappiness, but so it was.

'I want to take care of you, Sophie. If you'll let me.' She felt the deep breath he drew into his lungs. 'I don't want you to leave. I want you to stay, with Eleni and me. Always.'

No. It wasn't true.

'Marry me, Sophie?' His hand stroked her hair, gentle and almost tentative. 'Marry me and live here, with us?'

For an instant she felt burgeoning joy. And then it was quenched as she registered the implication of his words.

For a single, glorious moment she'd forgotten that Eleni was the sole reason he'd brought her to Greece. Eleni had to be the only reason he was proposing now. He loved his daughter and he'd do anything, even marry, to make the little girl happy.

'No,' she whispered when she found her voice.

'No!' His voice was a muted roar. So much for his unaccustomed humility. 'What are you saying?'

'There's nothing between us,' she said and pulled herself away from him. He loosened his hold a fraction so she could sit up straight, but he wouldn't let her go. Typically stubborn. Well, she could be stubborn too.

'Nothing but sex.' She stared straight into his night-dark eyes as she said it, hoping he'd believe her.

'How can you say that?' His brows furrowed in a savage frown that highlighted the severe angles of his face.

'It's the truth.'

'You're lying, Sophie.'

Her gaze slid from his, down to the clean line of his jaw. 'You can't keep me here against my will indefinitely.'

'And what about Eleni? You would just leave her, because you are angry with me?'

'I…care for Eleni, very much. But you'll find someone else to look after her. You don't need me to do it.'

'You think I want to marry you so you can take care of Eleni?'

She shrugged, her eyes dropping from his jaw to the precise knot in his dark silk tie. 'It's convenient. Eleni likes me. And I remind her of her mother.' She let her glance skitter to his and then away again. Each word was bitter in her mouth as she forced herself to continue.

'No doubt I remind you of your wife. It's a neat solution from your perspective. But it's not what I want.'

Silence throbbed between them. Sophie held herself taut, perched on his lap, wishing against all common sense that he'd haul her close and tell her she was the only woman for him.

She really had a self-destructive streak where Costas was concerned.

'I should have told you about Fotini before,' he said in a deep voice that echoed hollowly between them.

'No!' That was the last thing she wanted to hear. 'There's no need to tell me.'

'There's every need.' His arms encircled her, hauling her close again. And, against her best intentions, she felt the heady delight of being held in his embrace. One last, tiny piece of paradise to enjoy before she left.

'That first day when you opened the door to me, it was as if I saw Fotini's ghost. The resemblance was remarkable.'

Sophie squeezed her eyes shut, pain slicing through her as he confirmed her fears.

'There were differences between you too. But in my mind I saw you as just like her.' He dragged in a deep breath, his chest pushing against her. 'That's why I refused to trust you at first.'

What? Sophie struggled to sit up straighter and meet his eyes, but his arms tightened like warm steel about her, locking her against his chest.

'I jumped to the conclusion that you'd been taking drugs. And when I told you about Eleni, when I offered you her legacy as payment to help her, that was my prejudice showing again.'

He'd been prejudiced *against* her because she reminded him of his wife? Sophie's mind buzzed with questions.

'It was only as I got to know you that I realised how wrong I was.' One hand circled her shoulder, caressing spiralling warmth into her rigid body. 'I found you were generous, caring. And honest.' He sighed, his breath a ripple of warmth through her hair.

'You were nothing like Fotini except in the most superficial of ways. And even that physical similarity faded as I yearned for you. Only you. For your bright eyes so fierce and passionate. For the touch of your hand.'

Dazed, Sophie heard the emotion in his voice, felt it in the tremor that ran through his body and in the brush of his hand on her shoulder. But she couldn't take it in.

'The night we kissed. *Christos!* That night I was terrified at how completely you made me lose control. I would have taken you right there in the hallway. I'd never experienced anything like it. I didn't trust myself not to ravish you. Every argument I'd used to keep my distance disintegrated once I held you in my arms. I had no defence against you. So I behaved brutally to push you away.'

His hand curled round the nape of her neck and pulled her in even closer. 'It was all I could do to prevent myself taking advantage of you.'

Taking advantage? That was how he'd seen their blaze of mutual passion?

Sophie struggled to loosen his embrace enough to sit back and look into his face. It was sombre, eyes dark with turbulent emotions.

'You insulted me, made me feel like a cheap tart, just because you didn't trust your libido?'

He winced as her words burst out. 'I couldn't trust myself to protect you any longer.'

'*Protect me?*' Her voice rose with outrage at the memory of her pain.

'And were you *protecting* me when you used me then shoved me aside later like something shameful? Were you protecting me when you accused me of planning an abortion? When you wanted me as a convenience in your bed?'

'You are right,' he said in a voice deep with shame. 'I am a man without honour. I have treated you appallingly.'

He drew in a tremendous breath and met her gaze. The emptiness, the ingrained despair she saw there, chilled her to the bone.

'I couldn't believe what I felt for you,' he said. 'It was beyond my experience and I reacted badly. I didn't want to believe what I felt. Tried to pretend I didn't believe in love.'

Love!

Was this some cruel joke?

'It was only after you rejected me yesterday, after I began to realise how much I'd hurt you and how much I needed you, that I began to understand.'

Sophie stared at his stern, commanding features, into his lost eyes, and felt her icy outrage disintegrate. He was hurting so badly. And she knew with absolute certainty that pain was not new to him. It was etched with the strength of years.

'Tell me about Fotini,' she whispered, realising at last that the past was the key to so much. She needed to understand what had happened to make Costas so distrustful.

He hesitated and she read the reluctance in his expression, the tight control.

'She was beautiful, spoiled, full of life,' he said in a low voice. 'It was a marriage of convenience, not love. I wanted a wife and she was pleased to accept me.'

His lips curved in a mirthless smile. 'There are some women who see me as a catch.'

Sophie ignored his last statement and shook her head, amazed at such a cold-blooded approach to choosing a life partner. Apparently her grandfather hadn't been alone in his belief that marriage and love had nothing to do with each other.

'It seemed enough at the time, Sophie,' Costas murmured. 'But then I hadn't met you.'

Dazed, she stared back at him. Her body reverberated with the force of the electric connection that sparked between them when he looked at her like that.

Hope surged within her.

'Fotini liked being the centre of attention. She was used to parties and fun. To an extravagant lifestyle.'

Sophie watched his brow furrow deep as he remembered. She wanted desperately to ease his hurt.

'When Eleni was born I thought it would help Fotini to settle into married life, give her a purpose that had been lacking in her life: someone other than herself to care for.'

And what about her husband? She hadn't cared for him?

Sophie found herself wondering why her cousin had married. Originally she'd assumed it was because Fotini was in love. Costas was sexy, overwhelmingly masculine, the sort of man any woman would want for herself. But he was also megawealthy. Now she wondered if that had been a factor in Fotini's decision to wed.

'But Fotini suffered from severe depression. And she didn't want our daughter.'

Costas turned his head to meet her gaze as her gasp of indrawn breath stretched between them. 'Her condition was so serious she was hospitalised. And when she came home, despite the medication, her moods were unpredictable, her behaviour extreme. The highest of highs and the darkest of lows.' He paused, nostrils flared and jaw set.

'The only constant was that she steadfastly refused to have anything to do with Eleni unless forced to.'

Sophie's heart clenched. For a little motherless child. For Costas, coping with a baby and a wildly unstable wife. And for her cousin, Fotini. What must they all have suffered?

'It turned out that Fotini's condition was exacerbated by the alcohol and the drugs her friends had been secretly supplying.'

'You're joking!' No one could be that foolish, surely.

He shook his head. 'I don't think they realised how serious her condition was. Fotini could be the life and soul of the party when the mood took her. But the night she died they found a mix of alcohol and illegal drugs in her bloodstream. That was why she ran off the road. We were just lucky no one else was with her at the time.'

'Oh, Costas.' Sophie curved her palm around the clenched tension in his jaw, wishing she could ease the pain that throbbed in his voice. The regret.

'It's over now,' he said, looking into her eyes. 'But you need to know I wasn't attracted to you because of any resemblance to Fotini. I want you for yourself, *glikia mou*. Everything about you is unique. You fill my heart in a way I never believed possible before.'

She met his eyes and saw the blaze of raw emotion there.

His hands cupped her face. She felt them shake. Those big, capable, powerful hands, trembling against her skin.

'I love you, Sophie. That's why I can't let you leave me. I want you with me always. I need you. You're part of me, part of my soul.'

Sophie closed her eyes for an instant against the hot, bright welling emotions that seared her. She was almost too scared to believe this was real.

'*Agapi mou.* I hurt you, I know. It was unforgivable. The act of a beast.' His ragged voice broke through the last of her barriers. 'What I feel for you—it scared me. Can you believe that? So like a coward I tried to run away, to pretend it was only lust between us.'

His thumb brushed her cheek in a soothing caress at odds with the searing fire in his eyes.

'I didn't believe in such a love between a man and a woman.' He shrugged. 'Perhaps it was the experience of an unhappy marriage. Or maybe it was fear of losing control, of total dependence on a single woman for my happiness. I don't know, Sophie. All I know is that I refused to believe what I felt. I lied to you and to myself, pretending it was something I could contain. But it was too late. And when you rejected me—' his voice deepened in pain and his hold on her tightened '—I lashed out at you. Unforgivably.'

Her eyes were brimful of tears. He was a dark blur filling her vision. She shook her head, too choked to speak. But her hands spanned his jaw, slid lovingly over his cheeks, his lips, his brow, needing the sensation of his hot flesh to anchor her in this spinning world of sudden, blazing happiness.

She leaned close. 'I love you too, Costas. So much. I tried to hide it from you—it was tearing me apart to leave you.'

'Sophie!' His voice, like black velvet, caressed her. 'We'll never be apart again, I promise.'

And then she couldn't speak, but this time because his lips were on hers, tenderly urgent. She opened for him and the world spun away.

It was an age later that she surfaced, panting as she dragged in oxygen. She felt so different. As if the shadows of the past had been banished by the magic of what she and Costas shared.

She smiled up into his face and he responded with a blazing grin that lit his features in a way that sucked the newly acquired oxygen straight from her lungs. He really was gorgeous when he looked at her like that.

'You've sealed your fate, Sophie. You're mine now.' There was no doubting the possessive gleam in his eyes. And Sophie didn't mind one bit.

She stroked the hard angle of his jaw, revelling in the sensation of his warm skin against hers.

'And you're mine.' She smiled and watched him swallow as she feathered her fingertips over his mouth.

'Sophie? There's something else you need to know.'

She experienced a moment's dread as she read uncertainty in his dark eyes. Then she squared her shoulders. Whatever it was, she could cope, now that she knew he loved her.

'What is it?'

'Eleni. She—'

'You said she was making a good recovery!'

'She is. The doctors are astounded at how well she's doing. The prognosis is very good.' He paused and she saw the pulse at the base of his neck quicken.

'The reason you were the only compatible donor we could find...' He hesitated and Sophie curled her fingers around his hand.

'When we did the initial blood tests the doctors discovered that no one in my family would be a match. Fotini was pregnant before we married. Eleni is no blood relation of mine.'

His dark gaze met hers and she read the question in it. 'Nevertheless I am her father. I love her and she will always be my daughter.'

For a long moment Sophie sat in stunned silence, absorbing the implications of his words. The story of deceit, betrayal and, above all, love.

What a man her Costas was! How strong. How generous and loving.

'All that matters is that you love me, *Costa mou*, just as I love you.'

'And you'll marry me? You'll even take on another woman's child?' There was an anguished edge to his voice and she knew it was uncertainty that held him so unforgivingly in its grip. Sophie slid her hands to his broad shoulders, massaging at the tightness there.

'Eleni will be *our* daughter,' she corrected.

He stared back, his face a sombre mask of slashing, powerful lines, his eyes burnished bright by emotion.

'I don't deserve you, Sophie. I know that. But I will spend my life making you happy.'

He smiled slowly, in a way that sent a skitter of excitement through her. She read mischief in the sudden twinkle of black eyes. 'And I will take enormous care to ensure you never change your mind. Starting immediately.'

He slid his hands round to the front of her shirt, his fingers deft and quick as they flicked open each button in turn.

'Costas—no!' She darted an appalled glance over his shoulder, fearful of seeing someone, Yiorgos maybe, outside the car. But the glade was deserted, except for some bird trilling in the shadows of the ancient olive trees.

Costas grinned as he slipped her shirt from her shoulders in a single, easy move and reached for the clasp of her bra.

'Sophie—yes!' He nuzzled at her breasts as he stripped her bra away and took her warm flesh in his hands. 'Yes and yes and yes!'

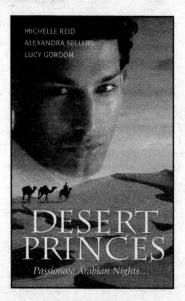

4 FREE

BOOKS AND A SURPRISE GIFT!

We would like to take this opportunity to thank you for reading this Mills & Boon® book by offering you the chance to take FOUR more specially selected titles from the Modern Romance™ series absolutely FREE! We're also making this offer to introduce you to the benefits of the Mills & Boon® Reader Service™—

- ★ FREE home delivery
- ★ FREE gifts and competitions
- ★ FREE monthly Newsletter
- ★ Exclusive Reader Service offers
- ★ Books available before they're in the shops

Accepting these FREE books and gift places you under no obligation to buy, you may cancel at any time, even after receiving your free shipment. Simply complete your details below and return the entire page to the address below. You don't even need a stamp!

YES! Please send me 4 free Modern Romance books and a surprise gift. I understand that unless you hear from me, I will receive 6 superb new titles every month for just £2.80 each, postage and packing free. I am under no obligation to purchase any books and may cancel my subscription at any time. The free books and gift will be mine to keep in any case.

P7ZED

Ms/Mrs/Miss/Mr ....Initials ....

BLOCK CAPITALS PLEASE

Surname ....

Address ....

....

....Postcode..............................

Send this whole page to:
UK: FREEPOST CN81, Croydon, CR9 3WZ